I0684514

The Voyagers Series

~ Africa ~

Will D. Rhame

The Voyagers Series – Africa

by Will D. Rhame

author@thevoyagers.net

No portion of this publication may be reproduced, stored in a retrieval system, or transmitted in any form or by any means without the prior written permission of the publisher.

www.thevoyagers.net

www.thevoyagersseries.com

Lexile: 1020L

Copyright © 2011 by Will D. Rhame

All rights reserved

ISBN: 10 0984974520

ISBN: 13 9780984974528

Printed in the United States of America

A New Approach to Reading and Retention

Let the Adventure Begin!

This book is dedicated to my wife,

Anna Katrina

and my three daughters –

Shyla, **Arlee**, and **Mauree**.

Special dedication to **Mrs. Jean Ann Rhame**, whose unconditional support made this project possible.

The Voyagers Series

ACKNOWLEDGMENTS

The Voyagers Series would not have been possible without the expert contributions of the following collaborators. I extend my deepest gratitude to each one.

Howard S. Harris, Attorney – Legal counselor

Orville H. Huseby, Attorney – Legal counselor

Barbara Sealund – Originator of the online games

Donna Massa-Chappee – Illustrator

Dr. Ken Christensen – Original website developer

John Davidson, CPA – Accountant

Dr. Gayani Leonard – Supporter

Peter L. Alcivar – Webmaster

Job Leyve – Graphic designer

Gino Legaspi – Composer

Linda Rooks – Editor

Illustrations

by

Donna Massa-Chappee

Table of Contents

CHAPTER 1

"**Book 1, Europe** was unbelievable!" exclaimed Drew as he and his sister talked over breakfast. "I can't wait to read the second book in the series."

"It's been our mode of travel until we reach eighteen!" Erin answered with equal glee. I know that Dad's stories got us both hooked on the idea of voyaging around the world, and I can't help but wonder if the adventures in these books will take us to every continent. I have looked up almost everything on the internet that was referenced in **Book 1, Europe**, and all of it was confirmed — the places, the cultures, the traditions, and even the clothes!"

"Yes, and in each chapter, there was a personal lesson that really spoke to us," Drew added.

"You might say that these are character-building travel passes!" Erin said with a laugh.

"Right, but we need to keep this quiet, Erin. If others found out about our cave and something was to happen to the books, we would lose our tickets to learn all this cool stuff."

"I agree," said Erin, "But perhaps after we finish the first book, we should talk about what to do next."

"Okay, but right now I want to take another vacation! Let's go!" Drew said as their mother entered the kitchen.

"Just a moment, you two! Where do you think you are going? You have chores to do. Come on now! Let's be quick about it," Jean said.

"Hey, Drew," Erin whispered, "After the chores, I'll meet

you behind the house."

"See you in a few. Then I'll race you to the forest!" Drew challenged.

"I heard that," Jean said. "I'm getting a little concerned about both of you spending so much time in the forest. What about your tennis?"

"Come on, Mom! It's summer vacation. Last week, I said that we would enter the next tennis tournament, remember?" Drew pleaded.

"Well, alright this time. You've only been out of school for a few days, but be careful. When will you be back?"

"Just in time for another one of your great suppers!" Erin said.

"What do you do out there all day?" Jean asked.

"We follow trails and talk about what it would be like to travel to some of the places that Dad has told us about," Drew said in a hurry.

"Okay, see you at supper time," Jean agreed.

With the chores finished and their run to the cave leaving them breathless, Erin said, "I'm glad that we agreed not to peek into the second book as we returned **Book 1, Europe** to its place last time."

"Yes, Erin, but the wait is over," Drew said as they walked up to the old trunk. "We knew that it had no writing on its leather cover, so I'll let you have the honor of opening it!"

As she carefully lifted the cover, Erin said, "Let's see where we are voyaging next!" To their delight, the inscription on the first page read, "**Book 2, Africa**."

~ Book 2, Africa ~

The Lion

It was a hot day when we arrived at the port of Mombasa. The year was 1788, and it had taken us six weeks to sail from our home in Darwin. Neither my brother, David, or I wanted to go on this trip, but our father had insisted. He was getting older, and he said that he wanted to teach us his business. We had lived well in Darwin over the years, but we had never inquired as to how Father made a living for our family.

He would leave for four months of the year, and when he returned, he always gave us little containers filled with finely-crushed melaleuca leaves. He taught us how to use them in a variety of ways. They could be rubbed into our skin, boiled in order to inhale the vapors, or placed on our tongues to mix with saliva and ingest. He instructed us as to the quantity of leaves that we should use if one of us got bitten by a poisonous creature, obtained a cut, or had some sort of stomach sickness. After years of using the leaves, we found that they really did help. So, we assumed that his business was solely in the selling of the healing melaleuca leaves.

Our father was a quiet man, and he never had discussed any aspect of his business with us. For all we knew, he could have been trading roos, but for whatever reason, we went along in his triple-mast wooden ship that felt like it would tip over at the slightest push of the wind. Fortunately, he always made us carry a small container of leaves, and I have to admit, they did prevent us from getting seasick.

David had just celebrated his fourteenth birthday, and a

few weeks earlier, I had turned fifteen. David was very strong and slightly taller than me. I loved my brother, and we got along very well. He enjoyed doing many things with his friends, but every once in a while, we would take a day hike together, and he would always look out for me.

It was night when we finally landed, and we had to stay onboard until morning. There were a number of ships like ours in the port. The strange thing was that David and I could hear moaning from time to time. It sounded like it was coming from some of the other ships, but we couldn't be sure. We were just excited to finally reach land and could hardly wait to get off the ship in the morning.

At sea, it had been hard to sleep because the hammocks would violently swing from side to side with the motion of the sea. In the harbor, there was very little movement, and sleep was peaceful and sound.

Our rest was soon broken, however, as David and I were awakened suddenly by the sound of men walking above us on deck.

"Arlee! Come on. Get up! Let's go ashore and check things out," David said as he jumped to his feet.

"Alright. I'll meet you up top in a minute," I replied.

When I made it to the upper deck, I saw my brother looking over the railing, and at first, I thought he had become ill, since the morning <u>temperature</u> was much higher than it would have been at home. When I got close enough to see his face, it was very pale, and his eyes were as large as those of a jumbuck.

"David, what's wrong?" I asked.

"Look at that, Arlee. If this is what Father does, I want no part of it. In fact, I want off this ship right now!" he said in disgust.

As I looked over to where he was pointing, I could see hundreds of black men in chains being whipped and forced to board several of the ships docked at the port. I couldn't believe my eyes! I grabbed David's hand, and we ran off Father's ship. The dock was crowded with many black men and a lesser number of women. It was a ghastly sight, and a feeling of sickness, combined with anger, began to rise in my stomach.

"David, if Father wants us to take over his business, then I don't want any part of it either. We need to get away from here as quickly as possible. I would rather run away from Father than help him do this. Let's go inland to hide out for awhile and then see if we can find another ship to take us back home," I said as tears began to stream down my face.

David put his arm around me as we left the dock area and started walking deeper and deeper into a land we knew nothing about.

After three days of non-stop walking, we began to see a landscape that was made up of tall dry grasses, rolling hills, bushes, and a few trees. We were able to see far in the distance, and in one direction, we saw clouds that were producing rain. We had heard someone on Father's ship say something about the savanna, and we supposed that this was it. Most of the area was devoid of green grass, and instead, the meter-high dry grass was yellow in color. It appeared that there had been no rain for months in this area. In another direction, we saw an extremely large mountain, surrounded by a dense jungle. The jungle extended far into the savanna on the left side near the base of the mountain. We began to notice large herds of animals, all walking in the same direction. It was a surreal sight that seemed like a dream.

"I'm so thirsty, and I need to rest," I said.

Then, it hit me like a ute. In a fit of anger, I had led my brother deep into this foreign land with only a bow and arrows on my back and the sword that David carried. We each had bota bags that were about half full of water and our small containers filled with crushed melaleuca leaves that our father always made us carry.

"David, I think I made a mistake. Perhaps we should turn around right now and see if we can find our way back to the port."

"You made no mistake, Arlee. This was my idea too, and I want you to stop thinking that you have to make all of the decisions. We've got to be a team, and all of our decisions need to be made together, you dag!"

With that, we broke out laughing, but each of us was well aware that our situation was serious. As we quieted down, we heard a strange and haunting moan that was coming from the west. There, about a hundred meters in front of us, was something big. "Do you see that hairy thing? It's just lying there. Do you want to check it out?" I asked.

David cleared his throat and said, "Yes, but as soon as we see what it is, we need to start heading back."

"Sounds good," I said enthusiastically.

Cautiously, we started to walk toward the hairy figure, and the closer we got, the larger the figure became. I grabbed David's arm as we approached what appeared to be a huge white cat. The cat didn't move. It didn't even look at us. It just moaned. We walked closer and saw that the right front foot of this huge beast was caught in a snare. It had caused great swelling, and blood was all around it. The cat was dying.

"We can't just leave it here, David. We must try to help! I can't stand to hear it moaning!" I said, sobbing.

We both knew what had to be done. David looked at me, and I nodded my head. He took out his knife, and with every part of his body shaking, he slowly walked up to the impressive beast. The cat was incredibly large, and David jumped back when it moaned again. For some reason, I wasn't scared at all. In fact, I was already behind the cat, stroking its massive head. The cat had a thick mane covering his neck and chest. His hair was pure white, and a thick tuft of it covered the end of his tail. His paws appeared to be about thirty centimeters across, and when he moaned, we saw two teeth that were approximately fifteen centimeters long.

David knelt down next to the cat's injured paw. The huge animal did not move. As David looked at the big cat's eyes, the ensnared beast maintained a dull stare into space, seemingly ready to accept his fate. With his knife in hand, David carefully began to move the hair around on the cat's massive paw. The animal kept perfectly still. The swelling had covered up most the snare.

"I'm going to have to cut into his skin to remove the snare," David said.

"It's alright, David. He is a proud and strong male, but he's in great need of help. I believe he will not harm you," I said, continuing to pet the cat's head.

David hesitated for a moment but then began to cut. The massive cat tensed but made no movement. Soon, David was able free the cat's paw from the snare.

I gave the cat some water to drink from my bota bag, and then I mixed a bit of water into some crushed melaleuca leaves and sprinkled the mixture on the wound. We knew very well that it had always stopped the pain and allowed quick healing whenever we had been wounded. Both of us stepped back, and within a few minutes, the cat's eyes began to blink. When he opened them fully, they gleamed a dark blue.

David and I smiled broadly at each other. It seemed to have been a job well done! Suddenly, the massive cat picked up his head and looked at us with what appeared to be a questioning stare. The cat gingerly rose up to test his wounded paw. He stood almost two meters tall at his head, and although he was thin because he had not been able to eat, he still was massive. David and I saw the solid muscles in his legs, and his impressive mane was so thick that we could barely see his round ears. The cat yawned, and for the first time, we saw the incredible size of his jaws. His mouth opened so wide that one of our heads could easily have fit into it. We stood there and stared at him. We were so close that neither of us would have had time to defend ourselves if he had decided to attack.

"He is not going to hurt us, David. Stay still, and look away from his eyes," I said softly.

David knew that I had a special way with animals, and he did as I said. The great cat looked at us and then turned his head from side to side. In one quick motion, he took two steps toward me and rubbed his <u>enormous</u> head against my stomach and then licked my hand. He almost knocked me down in doing so. Then, the big cat did the same thing to David. After his display of affection, he laid back down, inviting us to play with him.

Without hesitation, I walked over to the cat and began to scratch his back. David followed cautiously, probably thinking that I had lost my mind! As we petted the cat, we were overwhelmed by his strength yet surprised by his gentleness toward us. Soon, we forgot about the danger and were simply enthralled with this giant white cat. We rolled around and played with him until the huge animal jumped up suddenly. His ears folded back as he turned his head to listen to what was behind him. In an instant, his finger-length claws grabbed the savanna floor, and with a thunderous, distinctive roar, he took off running.

David and I looked at each other, totally stunned. We had never heard a roar that loud in our lives. Just as I was wondering why the cat had left, we were surrounded by six black men, holding a variety of spears, clubs, and animal-hide shields. We knew better than to take out our weapons. We just stood back-to-back, looking at the men. The warriors must have seen us playing with the huge white lion, and they seemed fearful of us.

The warriors were dressed in red cloth skirts with white bands of cloth around their midsections that looked similar to thick belts. Each man was adorned with several elaborate necklaces. The necklaces appeared to be made of variously-colored beads and other materials. Some of the men had what looked like strings of red and blue beads mixed with small white seashells that extended from their necks and crisscrossed down their chests. Some wore white cloths on top of their heads, while others had braided hair and brightly-colored headdresses. One of the men wore a headband that had a bronze figure in the middle. The men were also wearing bracelets that looked similar to their necklaces. Some were carrying spears that had intricate designs painted on the shafts, while others had heavy wooden clubs with fist-sized rocks attached to one end. Each warrior carried an oval-shaped shield that was covered with different types of animal hides. The men had distinctive-looking faces, and all of them were in great physical condition. Their appearance and behavior reflected a great sense of pride.

It was readily apparent to us which of the men was the head warrior. He took a step closer to David and said, "*Ambapo ni kutoka kwa*?" (Where are you from?). David just stood still, not understanding. The same warrior said, "*Wat ni jina yako*?" (What is your name?).

Neither of us had any idea what he was saying. Here we were in his country, and we could not show respect by communicating with him. Finally, David said, "We were just about to leave," nodding respectfully.

Together, we took a step back from the men, but the head warrior, who was also acting as the lead warrior at the front of the column, said, "*Hakuna!*" (No!) "*Kuacha!*" (Stop!), slamming his spear into the ground in front of us. The other warriors responded by surrounding us and pointing their spears at our stomachs.

The lead warrior spoke to his men, and they all seemed to agree. Then he pulled his spear up from the ground and pointed it in the direction of the far-off mountain surrounded by jungles and said, "*Kwenda!*" (Go!). David and I looked at each other and understood that we were to follow them to the distant mountain. We had no choice. With three warriors in front of us and three behind, we took off for the mountain at a steady run. The warriors' <u>endurance</u> was amazing.

David and I realized that we had no chance of escape, so we tried to keep pace with the men. The heat from the enormous ball of fire in the sky beat down on us as we continued to run. It was grueling, but we were allowed to take periodic sips of water from our bota bags. The warriors ran in perfect unison with ease and grace, and each stride they took was the same. It would have been beautiful if we weren't being forced to run with them. The aggravating thing was that none of them showed any sign of being tired! Since were in fairly good shape from playing soccer back home, David and I were able to keep up with them throughout the day. The warriors seemed impressed that we withstood the challenge in spite of all the extra clothing and gear that we had.

We observed that the head warrior sometimes acted as the lead warrior and at other times he delegated the lead position to another of his men. They were a real team, and we were fascinated with their precision.

As we ran, we began to notice all kinds of unique animals that were <u>migrating</u> in the same direction. One of the warriors pointed to one very unusual animal as it bolted to join its herd, and said, "*Twiga.*" These animals had extremely long legs and incredibly long necks. Their hides were similar to brown squares outlined by thin white lines. They had two short horns sticking up from the tops of their heads and long tails with tufts of black hair at the ends. They must have been nearly six meters tall.

Another warrior pointed to one of the largest animals that we had ever seen and said, "*Tembo*." This animal was not as tall as those with the long necks, but it was much broader. The *tembo* was completely grey and had very large ears and a huge, long nose that it used almost like a hand. Its legs were as thick as tree trunks and its skin resembled wrinkled leather. A whole herd of these great animals slowly lumbered in the direction of the rain.

The variety of animals that we saw was staggering. It seemed that we were in a fantasy land filled with creatures of every size, color, and shape, yet there was no stopping to enjoy the view! The warriors continued their steady pace, and it took all of our strength to keep up.

When David suddenly came to a halt, bent over, and put his hands on his knees, I quickly dropped to the ground. But the lead warrior said to us, "*Hakuna*!" He pointed behind us, then turned and pointed in front of us again, saying, "*Kwenda*!" in a forceful tone of voice. We looked behind but saw nothing, so we both got up and continued to run.

"What are we running from?" I asked.

"I don't know, and I don't think I want to know," David said apprehensively.

Finally, the scorching sun began to fall from the sky and the relentless heat started to subside. We were finally getting closer to the jungle, but the mountain was still a distance away.

Before the sun slipped over the horizon, the lead warrior stopped and said a few words to the other men. David and I gratefully fell down, exhausted. Together, we uttered, "Thank you!" The lead warrior only looked at us and shook his head.

The rest of the warriors gathered sticks, branches, and wood. The lead warrior began to start a fire with a stick, rope, and log. Soon, he was able to produce a spark and a fire started. The warriors continued collecting what seemed like too much wood. The fire grew so large and hot that we had to move away from it, but the lead warrior only allowed us to retreat just far enough away to avoid getting burned.

Eventually, night enveloped the savanna and the warriors surrounded the fire. Four warriors sat, and two stood guard. David and I were so tired that we just sat in silence. The head warrior offered us some dried beef, and we ate it gladly.

Out of nowhere, we began to hear growls, screams, and the noise of hooves running in all directions. At first, the sounds seemed far off, but soon, they were coming closer and closer. David and I looked at each other in horror at the intensity of the animals' cries. As the commotion surrounded us, all of the warriors were standing, and three of them had sticks from the fire that were burning at one end. As they twirled the sticks around, the others were banging on their animal-hide shields. The animal sounds were fiercely aggressive. One kind of animal had a hideously-distinctive laughing sound. We were in the middle of a killing field where nothing was safe.

I stood up and tried to peer out onto the savanna ahead of us, but there was no moonlight, and all I encountered was total darkness. As I looked in the direction from which we had come, I could just barely make out another campfire. I sat down quickly and huddled next to David. I was shaking uncontrollably, and he must have seen the terror in my eyes.

"David, there's another campfire back there! I think we are being followed!"

"Well, Arlee, that explains a lot. We are with men who know what they are doing," David said, trying to mask his own fear. "At least we have learned why we have been running so fast."

As I looked at the warriors, tears began to well up in my eyes. The savagery was agonizing to hear, and our only chance of survival was the fire and the warriors who were keeping the predators away. Never in our experience had we ever felt so scared or helpless.

Seeing my tears, David interjected, "Arlee, we must control our fear. What is the worst that could happen? We get eaten alive!"

I could have hit him, but instead, I started to laugh. "David, you always crack a joke at the worst moments, but tonight, I'm glad you did."

The sounds of the animals in the savanna were so loud that it was hard to think about anything else, but I began to notice something extraordinary about the warriors. Even though they were fully involved in standing their ground against the animals, they seemed calm. I wondered if they had done this hundreds of times before.

David and I huddled close together as we continued to watch the warriors that were protecting us. I'm not sure if either of us got much rest, but the night finally passed, and almost as suddenly as it started, the savanna settled down. The light of the rising sun began to illuminate the beautiful land.

In a tired but kind voice, the lead warrior said, "*Gani*?" (How are you?) Realizing that we didn't understand, he simply pointed to the big mountain and said, "*Tafadhali*" (Please).

David and I understood what he wanted, and we arose, glad to be on our way. The lead warrior gave us another piece of dried meat, and we set off. Now that we knew why the head warrior insisted upon running, it made it easier to keep pace.

As we found our stride, we saw more unusual animals. This time, I tapped the warrior in front of me and pointed to one of the animals. The warrior smiled and said, "*Kifaru.*"

The *kifaru* was grey in color and appeared to be covered in some sort of armored skin, with one long, sharp horn on the front of its nose and a smaller one behind it. Although the *kifaru* looked enormous, it was able to run surprisingly fast. It stood about two meters high and four meters long. We were amazed at the features of this mighty animal.

The heat of the savanna was stifling, but the intense pace continued. Finally, as the sun moved to the top of the sky, we began to see the details of the jungle ahead of us. It was extremely lush, with green vines and tall trees that we hoped would offer relief from the hot, arid savanna. We felt a sense of anticipation, believing that we finally were going to get some shade.

It didn't take long for us to reach the jungle, and when we entered, the pace of the warriors slowed. Grateful to be walking, we noticed that the oldest warrior had been designated by the head warrior to take the lead. He was smaller than the other men, and his spear was much longer, being nearly four meters in length. He carefully guided the column into a jungle so thick that it seemed impossible that it could be penetrated at all. We perceived that his experience in the jungle was highly respected by all of the warriors.

Our hope of a cooler temperature was not to be realized. Not only was it nearly as hot in the jungle, it was also extremely humid. The sun was occluded, which was a great relief, but the humidity caused us to sweat profusely. The only reprieve was that we were moving more slowly. Walking was easier than running, but the path was much harder to negotiate. We followed the lead warrior and were amazed that he was able to find any trail at all.

After some time, the lead warrior stopped at a small opening in the forest. He pointed to what looked like some kind of deer on the other side of the opening, and then he pointed to something on a large branch above it. The other warriors were quiet as they watched the deer. In a flash, a huge, multi-colored snake fell from the branch directly over the deer. It wrapped itself around its helpless prey. The deer fell, and the snake began to squeeze it when it exhaled. I could hardly watch. Shortly thereafter, when the deer had suffocated, the gigantic snake undertook the grizzly job of eating it whole.

The size and power of the snake was incredible. David and I looked at each other in disbelief as the lead warrior took us around the gorging snake. We continued to follow the elder warrior over dead trees and around thick vines. He always kept his long spear touching the ground in front of him as though he were blind.

Soon, we understood why he moved his long spear from side to side in his path. As he advanced, the spear was bitten by another snake that blended in with the jungle floor so well that it was impossible to visually detect. The warrior behind the leader quickly jumped out in front and beat the snake to death.

As we continued on what seemed like an invisible path, the warrior who was now at the front stopped and shouted something to the head warrior. The head warrior left his position near us to go to the front of the column once again. He then motioned David and I to come up next to him. He took his spear and moved a quantity of leaves and twigs. Underneath were thousands of huge ants that were running incredibly fast in a straight line. The ants were carrying pieces of the bodies of insects, snakes, and rodents. The head warrior shook his head and said, "*Siafu*." David and I had learned about army ants in school, and to our amazement, we were now looking at them!

As we resumed forward motion, two of the warriors ran ahead of the group. Soon, they came back with big smiles on their faces. They were carrying a dead monkey. A couple of the other warriors built a fire and began to roast the animal. After awhile, they began tearing it apart and offered pieces of meat to everyone. I felt sick to my stomach and declined it. David decided to try it and said that it tasted good. He encouraged me to eat. I forced myself to do so, knowing that if I didn't, I would not have the strength to continue through the jungle. To my surprise, I felt better.

We were increasingly appreciative of the warriors who were caring for us. We had seen and heard some of the most terrifying things in our lives in this strange and beautiful land, yet the warriors had shown great respect for each other and for both the savanna and the jungle. They killed animals only to survive, and they shared what little they had with us. They always appeared to be happy. This was their way of life, and we observed their sense of accomplishment at being able to cope with the elements.

In the searing heat of day, we saw a land that had a beauty

we could never have imagined. The insects, reptiles, birds, rodents, and predatory animals all had their special places here. We began to understand that the keys to human survival amongst them were knowledge, respect, and awareness.

As we traveled through the jungle, the warriors began to sing, rhythmically tapping their spears against their shields. It was a beautiful melody that truly charmed us. The head warrior sang, and the other warriors echoed him in unison.

With the sun nearing the horizon, another large fire was lit, and David and I braced for nightfall.

CHAPTER QUESTIONS

1. Where is Africa located on a world map?

2. What bodies of water surround Africa?

3. In what country is Mt. Kilimanjaro located?

4. Are white lions albinos?

5. Why is the savanna so dangerous?

6. What is a poacher?

7. What are the most well-known animals in Africa?

8. How long, in feet, is the lead warrior's spear?

9. What African countries surround Kenya?

10. What is the capital of Kenya?

TRIVIA QUESTION

What is the population of Africa?

CROSSWORD PUZZLES & GAMES

www.thevoyagers.net

Now that you have read the Chapter, answered the Chapter Questions, and researched the Trivia Question, it's time to go to our website! Click the PUZZLES tab and follow the directions. Remember, the underlined words in the chapter are the answers to the online CROSSWORD PUZZLE! You may want to write them down, as one of them is your CODE to play the online GAME!

HAVE FUN!

CHAPTER 2

"Drew, there is no way a snake can eat a deer whole," Erin said emphatically.

"Let's go outside the cave so we can get a connection and look it up on the web through our cell phones. I think there are such snakes," Drew replied.

"Okay, you look that up, and I'll see if there are really white lions in Africa," Erin said as she took her phone out of her pocket.

"Listen to this!" Drew said. "African rock pythons can grow up to six meters and weigh up to fifty-five kilograms. These constrictors are the largest snakes in Africa, and it is true that they swallow their prey whole after asphyxiation. A python captures with its sharp teeth and then coils around its prey. It squeezes tighter as the prey exhales, making it impossible to take another breath. The python's prey includes large rodents, deer, and even crocodiles! Can you imagine?"

"That's disgusting!" Erin said, looking squeamish.

"What about the white lions?" Drew asked.

"This is really interesting!" Erin said as she read the text from her phone. "White lions are not albinos. They have a rare color mutation that is often revered in African culture."

"We are learning a lot from this adventure! Come on. Let's read the next chapter. I can't wait to see what happens in the jungle!" Drew said as they went back into the cave.

~ Book 2, Africa ~

The Run

The fire began to burn in a jungle so dark that we could not see more than a few meters in front of us. Two of the warriors ventured out into the blackness and soon brought back what looked like a small deer, which they cooked over the fire. We were grateful to have something to eat. The nourishment, along with some of the water in our bota bags, made us feel energized. I had noticed that there were no visible wounds on the deer. I also noticed that one of the warriors had a straight round stick that was about one-and-a-half meters long, with one end slightly larger than the other.

I walked over to the warrior who was holding the stick and gestured to indicate that I would like to look at it. The warrior grabbed the stick tighter and glared back at me menacingly. The head warrior came up to the other warrior and said something in a <u>commanding</u> tone. The warrior begrudgingly handed the object to me. I bowed to the warrior to thank him for allowing me to look at it. It was beautifully carved, and as I examined it, I learned that I could look through one end of the stick and see out the other.

The lead warrior took the hollow stick from me and ordered the warrior who originally had it to give me a small pointed object. The lead warrior placed the object, pointed end first, into the hole at the larger end and raised the stick. He put his mouth onto the large end where the object was inserted and pointed the narrow end at a nearby tree. After taking a huge breath, he blew as hard as he could into the stick. The small pointed object ejected out of the other end, soaring at an amazing speed. It hit the exact center of the tree that he was aiming at. It happened so fast that it was hard to see the dart flying through the air. The other warrior retrieved the small dart from the tree and carefully put it back into a small leather sack that he had attached to his side.

Then, the head warrior gave the stick back to me and said some words to the other warrior, who then retrieved the dart from his pouch and handed it to the head warrior. The warrior grasped the large end of the dart in his right hand and looked at me. He pointed to the sharp end of the dart with his left hand, and shook his left forefinger over the top of the dart. He also shook his head in a way that indicated to me to be careful not to touch the pointed end. I realized that it was a poisonous dart.

As I held the long hollow stick, the warrior put the dart into the thick end. He extended his arm in the direction of the tree and invited me to try hitting the spot where he had landed his dart. I smiled in a playful manner and aimed the stick at the tree. I blew as hard as I could. The dart flew out of the other end and stuck into the tree just a few centimeters away from the spot that the head warrior had hit.

As all of the warriors looked at me with surprise, the head warrior smiled proudly. I was amazed at how efficient this device was, and although I could now understand why there were no marks on the deer, I still wondered where the warriors got the potent poison for the darts.

"Arlee, I wish I could communicate with these men. I have so many questions," I said.

"Yes, I would love to know where they are taking us and who is following us. Oh, David, I am so tired. I just want to go home," Arlee said. With that statement, we both laid down near the fire to get some sleep.

So far, the jungle had seemed so peaceful, and it was easy to fall asleep near the crackling fire with only the buzzing of many insects breaking the silence. But before long, I was jolted awake by the sound of Arlee's screams. The warriors had gathered around her, and there on her arm was the largest and hairiest spider that I had ever seen! One of the warriors chuckled, until he got a disapproving glare from his leader. The head warrior grabbed a flat stick and slowly put it in front of the spider. With his other hand, he gently held Arlee's shoulder so she would not make any sudden movements.

As the spider gingerly walked onto the stick, I noticed that it had eight finger-long, hairy legs and an abdomen the size of small tomato. Its head had eight black, beady eyes and two extremely large black fangs. In fact, the spider was completely black.

Although Arlee had been shaking with <u>fear</u> at first, her love of animals caused her to become interested in this bizarre-looking creature. The head warrior carefully took the spider to the other warrior who had laughed and put the stick and spider next to his face. Then he shook the stick. The spider reacted to the shaking of the stick, lifting its two front legs and raising its head to expose its twelve-millimeter-long fangs. The warrior backed off in horror, tripped, and fell down. The rest of the warriors laughed.

The head warrior turned to Arlee and said, "*Mbaya buibui*"

(Bad spider). In a display of <u>compassion</u>, he took the eight-legged monster back into the jungle and gently put it down. The spider crawled away, seemingly undaunted, back into its dark, foreboding home.

As Arlee and I watched the warrior return the spider back to its natural environment, we realized something more about the character of this man. Instead of destroying the spider, he let it go. He was respected by his fellow warriors, and the bond between them was obvious.

Each of the men knew his place within the group and they all worked together as a powerful team. They played when an opportunity presented itself, but their knowledge of their strange and wondrous homeland was vast, and they took survival seriously. The warriors had certainly taught us the importance of having a fire, not only for warmth and for cooking food, but as a visible barrier between us and the ever-present animals.

With the spider no longer a threat, Arlee said, "I think I love this place, David. My fear of the strange animals is turning into a deep desire to learn more."

"Are you crazy, Arlee? That spider could have bitten you! This is the scariest place we have ever been. There are so many ferocious animals that..." I paused and then said mockingly, "Oh, sure. I get it. This is an animal haven for you. You could study and connect with hundreds of different types of animals for the rest of your life!"

"David, just promise me one thing for now, Arlee said, graciously ignoring my sarcasm. "Stay close to the fire and our warrior friends."

"Warrior friends? They kidnapped us, Arlee!" I said in a high-pitched tone.

"Yes, I know, David. But look at it from their point of view. They are running from what may be a bad group of warriors. They also saw us playing with the big white cat, and they have acted in our best interest the entire time. You could even say that they have saved us!" Arlee said, looking straight into my eyes.

"Arlee, you always have a way of looking at a bad situation and finding the good in it. I see your point, and maybe you are right. I guess things could be worse. But all I want is to get back to the boat. I miss our home."

"I am focused on getting back, too," Arlee agreed.

"It seems that our lives have become a voyage, and we must learn to survive under various circumstances. The decisions we make will determine our future, and the better our decisions, the stronger we will become. They can kidnap us, but they cannot change the way we think or learn. We make the ultimate decisions, and right now, all I want to do is to stay alive in this creepy place," I said.

"David, are you getting philosophical with me?" Arlee joked. We both laughed, shook our heads, and were content to stay near the fire. The head warrior approached and handed each of us another piece of meat. Knowing that he was mindful of our needs, we felt relaxed.

After we ate, I asked Arlee to sit back-to-back so we could get some rest. She did so, and I leaned against her. With a tired voice, she said, "Thank you."

Later that night, the warrior who was watching over us gently touched my shoulder to wake me. As I looked up at him, he put his finger to his mouth, indicating that I should remain quiet. He then touched Arlee's shoulder, and when she opened her eyes, he waved his hands back and forth across each other to indicate that she should stay still. I glanced over my shoulder and saw that there was a large bug on Arlee's leather pants. It was about one hundred millimeters long and twelve millimeters around. It had hundreds of legs on each side of its round, hard body. I wanted to jump up, but I remembered the warning of the warrior, and both of us stayed seated.

The long multi-legged bug was walking half on Arlee's pants and half on her exposed leg. The warrior carefully took a small round stick and very slowly tried to put the stick under the head of the crawling bug. But the bug resisted going onto the stick as it used its numerous legs to grab onto her clothing and skin. The warrior could not get the stick under it.

The strange-looking bug must have sensed a potential attack, and it bit Arlee's leg. She screamed and jumped up, but it was too late. The bug had delivered its lethal poison. She slapped the bug off her leg, and the warrior killed it. Arlee held onto her leg as the poison began to enter her bloodstream and do its deadly work.

"David, it is so painful!" she cried out as I scrambled over to see if I could help.

The head warrior saw the whole thing and knew that the warrior who was watching over us had tried to do the right thing. Everyone was awake now, and the head warrior came over and motioned with his hands for everyone to step back so he could see where Arlee had been bitten. She showed him the spot.

The head warrior took out a rock that he carried in a pouch on his waist. He said something to the other warriors, and they grabbed me and moved me out of the way. Although I struggled, I soon realized that I could not escape from the larger and stronger warriors who were holding me. The head warrior wasted no time. Using the sharp end of the rock, he made a small cut over the bite on Arlee's leg. He put his mouth over the cut and began sucking the blood out of her leg and spitting it out onto the ground. She groaned but did not move.

Although she repeated that she was in terrible pain and was feeling sick, I knew that the head warrior was trying to help her. After I relaxed, they let me go. I went over to Arlee and held her hand. As she began to describe how ugly the long bug was, I noticed that her speech was beginning to slur. I knew that she was in grave danger from the terrible bite and that everything the warrior was doing might not work.

The warrior stood up and looked at me with a concerned expression. I saw that Arlee's condition was becoming more serious. Her skin was turning pale and her eyes were losing focus. Suddenly, I motioned with my hands and arms to have the warriors step aside, and they respectfully did so.

I had remembered the crushed melaleuca leaves that we carried, but I did not want the warriors to see them. I took the container of finely crushed leaves from my pouch, sprinkled it on Arlee's wound, and rubbed it in. In a matter of moments, Arlee said that the pain began to dissipate and that she had actually started to feel a little better. The combination of the head warrior's quick action in getting the affected blood out of her leg and the use of our crushed leaves was critical.

I whispered in Arlee's ear, telling her to relax for awhile but to remember to thank the head warrior later. She understood and nodded with a little smile. I walked over to the head warrior and extended my hand to thank him. The warrior did not understand the gesture, so I bowed instead. The warrior seemed to understand and mimicked me. To the amazement of all the warriors, Arlee was feeling well enough to stand up. She nodded graciously in the direction of the head warrior. He must have believed that it was his intervention that had saved her life. It could have been, but Arlee and I knew that the leaves had powerful healing properties.

Arlee and I resumed sitting back-to-back next to the fire. Before long, the pitch black night of the jungle was disturbed by shafts of dull light penetrating through the canopy of trees. Morning was approaching, and certainly none of us had gotten much sleep.

As soon as it was light, the head warrior stood up. He spoke to one of his men and then motioned us to get up. We soon began walking again. Arlee and I were both resigned to continue our trek with this band of brothers.

We realized just how important our crushed leaves were.

Extreme dangers lurked all around us, from the savanna to the jungle and from large animals to small, and each of our containers contained less than half of the <u>precious</u> leaves.

I looked into my sister's eyes and said in a determined tone, "Arlee, we must be careful to conserve our supply of leaves and not use them unless it is a life-or-death situation."

"I agree, David. We must be extremely alert to potential dangers. From now on, we should sleep in shifts."

"That is a good idea," I replied.

The jungle had proved to be a constant killing field, both day and night, whereas the savanna's primary upheaval was during the night. We were beginning to understand that the lessons of this land were ancient and simple. We needed to be constantly vigilant and ever mindful of the inherent dangers.

As we joined the warriors, we again proceeded along the seemingly <u>invisible</u> trail that the lead warrior was following. We were more aware of our surroundings than we had ever been, suspecting the potential threats from the creatures around us. It was a humble feeling, based on total respect. As our parents had taught us, we knew that we must use our minds to the fullest.

The lead warrior brought the column to a stop beside the steep bank of a river. "Be careful, Arlee! If you fall in, there is no way to climb out," I cautioned.

The river was about forty meters wide, but it appeared that it was becoming narrower as we walked along its banks. After traveling for some time, the river had narrowed to just ten meters in width. Both Arlee and I noticed some very large creatures in the water. It was hard to tell what they were, because the water was muddy and the creatures were submerged.

"I do not think I want to swim in these waters," I said to Arlee.

"No way! Did you see the size of those animals? Some

of them were as big as the two-horned animals that appeared to have armor!" I exclaimed, recalling the unusual species on the savanna.

One of the large, round animals rose out of the water and opened its mouth. We looked at each other in astonishment. The huge beast's mouth was so large that a child could stand up inside it. It had only a few teeth, but they were sizeable. The longest four were at least a meter in length. The creature made deep sounds that resembled quacking.

"I cannot believe how wide that animal can open its mouth! And look at how fast it runs in the water," I noted. "There are hundreds of them!"

Further along the river, we saw a muddy beach on the opposite side from where we were walking. Lying on the beach were several salties that were at about four meters long. They had huge heads, and when one of them opened its mouth, we saw fifty or more daggered teeth. Their legs were short compared to their immense bodies. They looked like the same kind of animals that we had back home, but these were much larger.

One of the warriors threw a stick at the salties, and we were amazed at how fast they ran into the water. Once there, they swam at incredible speeds and disappeared from sight. When their mouths snapped shut, we could hear loud cracking sounds.

Both types of beasts lived together in the river. It seemed to me that there was no place in this strange land that was safe.

"We started with the big creatures, then we dealt with the small, and now we are back with the big ones again. Good grief!" I said in exasperation. Arlee could not help but laugh.

The head warrior increased the pace, and we were soon jogging. Their endurance was incredible. I looked behind, and in the far distance, I saw the other group of warriors trying to catch up with us. I decided not to tell Arlee, as she was keeping an eye on the animals in the water and trying to maintain the pace set by the warriors.

The sun was now in the middle of the sky, and the lead warrior signaled for everyone to stop. Arlee and I saw that the river had narrowed even more, and at its narrowest point, an old tree had fallen across it. It was the only possible bridge that we had seen, but it appeared that it would be a precarious crossing. A sinking feeling began to gnaw at my stomach.

One of the warriors tentatively began walking on the fallen tree to cross the river. Below him were many jaw-snapping salties that watched every step he took. The going was tediously slow, but he finally was able to reach the other side. All the warriors shouted in celebration.

The tree was old and fragile. It was about a meter thick, but at the other side, it narrowed to about a half meter. It was difficult to balance on it while stepping onto the other side of the river bank. Fortunately, the banks were steep enough that the salties were not able to propel themselves far enough out of the water to grab someone off the bridge.

With the rest of the warriors having crossed, only the head warrior, Arlee, and I remained. One of the warriors had slipped during his crossing but was able to catch himself before he fell. Each time one of the warriors reached the other side, the other warriors sang in <u>unison</u>. It sounded like a cheer. The head warrior came to Arlee and pointed with his arm, signaling her to cross the bridge.

She was not sure of herself, so she asked me to go first.

"Okay, Arlee. I will go first, but take a look down the trail from where we came. In the distance, do you see the group of warriors who have been following us?"

"Oh, I can see them! Never mind. I will go first!" she said without any more hesitation.

"Do not look down at the salties in the river. Focus on the log and each step that you take. Keep your arms stretched out and your knees bent for balance," I encouraged.

As she took her first step, everyone was watching. She closed her eyes for a moment, took a deep breath, and headed across. Everyone shouted and sang when she made it!

Now the head warrior motioned for me to go. I had no problem negotiating across the fallen tree and made it to the other side in record time. But, as I took my last step, I heard the tree cracking beneath my feet. I knew that the head warrior would be crossing next, and I feared for his safety. I felt responsible for the head warrior because it was my weight that had caused the tree to crack.

The head warrior immediately began to walk across the fragile tree bridge. I stood on the other side at the top of the steep bank, watching the head warrior's every move. He was making good time, but when he made his final step, the tree snapped. He fell into the river, very close to the steep bank. The massive salties had been patiently waiting, and as the head warrior struggled to climb the bank, one particular salty was swimming at a determined pace toward him.

I immediately slid down the bank and unsheathed my sword. Holding on to the sharp end, I offered the handle to the head warrior. He grabbed the handle and began to pull himself up. His weight was pulling against me, and the sword began to cut deeply into my hands. In an effort to help, two of the other warriors held onto me from behind so I would not slip closer to the river. The giant reptile had other plans. It was swimming toward the head warrior with a singular purpose – its next meal. It was a frightening sight, and the head warrior was running out of time.

With the other warriors bracing me, I pulled as hard as I could to help the head warrior up onto the bank. My hands were bleeding, but I continued to grip the sword as the warrior got one of his legs out of the water. At the last second, he was able to get his other leg onto the bank, just as the hideous salty leaped up and snapped its mighty jaws shut, narrowly missing the head warrior's foot.

As the four of us scrambled to the top of the bank, everyone yelled triumphantly and jumped up and down with joy. The head warrior promptly examined my badly-cut hands, and the look on his face was one of pure gratitude. He lifted his finger in a motion that indicated to me that I should wait right there. He ran into the jungle and returned shortly with some leaves, berries, and mud. He crushed the leaves and berries together and made a paste that he mixed with the mud. He carefully applied the unusual concoction to my wounds.

At first, I felt tremendous pain, but in no time, the pain was gone. The head warrior then took two large leaves from some nearby bushes and yanked out two sections of thin vine. He put one leaf onto my right hand and tied the vine around the leaf to hold the muddy substance in place. He did the same thing with my left hand.

When he finished mending my wounds, he called his men together and said a few words to them. They lined up in two rows of three and began to sing. They jumped up and down, continuing to look straight at me. The head warrior sang a tune and the other warriors repeated the melody. I was a little embarrassed, but the warriors continued to praise me, so I just looked over at Arlee and winked.

CHAPTER QUESTIONS

1. Why is Africa so hot?

2. How do humans survive in Africa with so many dangerous animals?

3. Why is the building of a fire at night in the savanna so important?

4. How can you show compassion for animals?

5. What is the largest animal in Africa?

6. Why do animals kill?

7. Why should you never travel alone in Africa or anywhere?

8. How long, in inches, is the multi-legged bug that crawls on Arlee's leg?

9. Why do the warriors take Arlee and Rob with them?

10. How wide, in feet, is the river at the point of crossing over the tree bridge?

TRIVIA QUESTION

What is the strongest reptile in the world?

CROSSWORD PUZZLES & GAMES

www.thevoyagers.net

Now that you have read the Chapter, answered the Chapter Questions, and researched the Trivia Question, it's time to go to our website! Click the PUZZLES tab and follow the directions. Remember, the underlined words in the chapter are the answers to the online CROSSWORD PUZZLE! You may want to write them down, as one of them is your CODE to play the online GAME!

HAVE FUN!

CHAPTER 3

"Can you identify with Arlee?" Drew asked as Erin closed **Book 2, Africa**.

"Absolutely! I feel like I am a part of this adventure, just like I did with **Book 1, Europe**," Erin replied.

"Oh, guess what! I just realized that we are still wearing the fourteenth century British costumes that we borrowed from Dad's collection while we read the first book! I'll do some research on the internet tonight and then exchange these costumes for something that Arlee and David might have worn back in 1788 as they left Australia," Drew said enthusiastically.

"Great! I love dressing the part. It puts me in Arlee's shoes!" Erin said with a big grin.

"Speaking of shoes! We've got to lace up and get in some practice before the tennis tournament this weekend," Drew mentioned.

"I know, but I would rather be here," Erin concluded as she opened the trunk.

"Me too, but maybe it will take Mom's mind off us always coming out here. Eventually, she is going to want to know more about what we are doing, and Dad is also going to start asking questions about why I borrow different costumes," Drew said.

"It does seem that we will have to tell them at some point, but until then, let's keep it our secret," Erin replied.

"Okay. We'll take it a day at a time. Let's read one more chapter before heading back for supper. I'm going to be good and hungry! Do you know what Mom is cooking?"

~ Book 2, Africa ~

The Village

In the midst of the ceremonial dance of appreciation for David, an arrow hit the ground near me. The head warrior saw it and immediately stopped the dancing. He looked across the river. The warriors that had been chasing us were on the other side. They were yelling things and banging their spears against their shields in a threatening manner. Their shouting and taunting did not seem to faze the head warrior or the other men. With the tree bridge now floating downstream, there was no way for the opposing warriors to cross the river. The head warrior said a few words to his men and gestured to David and I to start walking into the jungle. None of the warriors in our group showed any arrogance or retaliation toward the warring group across the river. Although they had just barely escaped their aggression, they did not celebrate or taunt them in any way. They simply continued on into the jungle as though nothing had happened.

"These men do not let anything perturb them," David said. "I sure wish I knew where they are taking us."

"Yes, we will know soon, but did you see how angry those other warriors were?" I asked. "I think we are fortunate to have fallen into the hands of these men. The pursuing warriors were so hateful."

"There is so much animosity in the world," David answered. Father always said that hate was one of the worst traits in people. Why do people have to fight all the time? Is it fear, greed, or lack of understanding? We have learned that the incredible animals here animals only kill to survive, but people kill each other for things like land or money. These warriors have shown us that it is possible to shun evil and pursue good. In as much as it depends on us, we should promote getting along with one other."

I turned my head to nod at my brother but said nothing. I was deep in thought as we continued to walk in line with the warriors. After several hundred meters of trekking, I said, "I agree with you, David, about the pervasiveness of hatred. People with different backgrounds and skin colors hate each other, people with different languages hate each other, and even people with the same language or skin color hate each other. We must strive to be of sound mind and base our attitudes and actions on respect for others. The last thing we want to do is add to the problem."

We continued to follow the lead warrior as he used his long spear to safeguard the way through the almost <u>impenetrable</u> jungle. Without the fear of the other warriors chasing them, the pace had slowed, and some of the warriors began talking among themselves. The jungle was so beautiful with its many different plants, trees, vines, and flowers, but David and I had to remind ourselves that, above all, it was dangerous.

As the sun reached the middle of the sky, the lead warrior stopped and motioned everyone to kneel down. About fifty meters ahead, we saw three huge, grey animals walking slowly and using their long noses to gather lush plants and place them into their mouths. The head warrior crept up to us and pointed at one of the animals. He said, "*Tembo.*"

Each *tembo* had ears that were a meter across and legs that were as big as tree trunks. The animals stood about three and a half meters tall and seemed rather gentle because of their slow and graceful stride. But since all of the warriors were kneeling down to hide, we knew that the creatures must be a potential threat.

The head warrior pointed up in the air and looked around. He waved his hands in the opposite direction of the animals. David said, "I think he is indicating that we are downwind of the herd."

"Yes, they cannot smell us, and from the way the warriors are acting, that is a good thing. We need to remember that, David," I said with conviction.

Everyone watched the mighty animals methodically walk a path they must have walked many times before. To my delight, I saw a baby *tembo* waking right next to its mother. It amazed me that the mother *tembo* was very careful to avoid stepping on her baby.

"For such large animals, they seem to be so sensitive," I said to David.

"Yes, but I would hate to get in their way. Did you see the *tembo* that had the curved white poles sticking out of its mouth? A hit from one of those things and it would be all over," David said quietly.

Finally, the herd moved on, and the lead warrior stood up and began his tireless walk toward a place yet unknown to us. The jungle was becoming even more dense, and the canopy of the trees almost totally blocked the light of the sun. However, we could see a more noticeable path heading into this deepest and darkest part of the jungle. Because David and I were both hoping that we were getting close to our destination, we thought that the more trodden path might be a good sign, but suddenly, the lead warrior stopped.

The head warrior, in a low and quiet voice, called all of the warriors together. They whispered to each other for a moment, and then two of them approached us. The two warriors stood in such a way that my brother and I were between them. They held their shields to the outside of their bodies as if to protect us as we walked. The head warrior and lead warrior were side-by-side at the front of the line and their shields were also held to each side. The head warrior said something and everyone began running swiftly down the dark path.

As we kept pace, David and I were totally confused. We had no idea why we were running between the two warriors and why their shields were up as if to protect us. We were both trying to peer into the jungle, but it was so dark that we could barely see anything. Then, we heard a number of thuds. Something was hitting the warriors' shields. David said he thought he saw a number of small children on both sides of us. Although I did not see anyone, the thuds continued to resound off the warriors' shields as we kept running along the path.

After a prolonged run, the jungle began to open up again, and a little more light from the sun found its way through the canopy. The warriors slowed down to a walk and moved into single file again. The warriors turned their shields around and carefully pulled out what looked like little darts that had stuck into the outside of their shields. The lead warrior continued to make his way down the more hidden path.

With the increased light, David and I were able to see further into the jungle. All we saw were trees, vines, and plants. I said to David, "What do you think that was all about?"

"I do not know. A few times, I thought I saw small children back there, but in the blink of an eye, they were gone!"

"Children? In that thick jungle? Have you lost your mind? Did you see the darts that the warriors removed from their shields? What children would do that?" I asked apprehensively.

"I have no idea, Arlee, but I hope we do not have to go back there again. That really scared me," David admitted.

The lead warrior stopped again, but this time he pointed to something in a large tree far in the distance. He continued on a course that veered slightly away from the tree. After walking about twenty-five meters, the head warrior pointed to a long bare limb on the same tree that the lead warrior had first pointing out. David and I looked at what was on it in astonishment. The head warrior said, "_Chui_." It was a magnificent spotted cat, lying on the branch with its legs dangling down on both sides. His big head was comfortably perched on the limb as he stared back at us. The cat seemed perfectly calm as he watched our column make its way through the jungle.

"That cat has the most beautiful coat I have ever seen! The black spots really stand out against its yellow and white fur. It has such gorgeous gold eyes and an extremely long tail. With the size of its paws, it looks so powerful, and yet it is totally serene, lying there in the tree," I said, transfixed with the cat's beauty.

The cat yawned and showed its huge fangs. "I would not want to play cat and mouse with it," David said with a chuckle. I was not amused.

After having run frantically through the savanna and then again through the darkest part of the jungle, David and I enjoyed the slower pace that was being set by the lead warrior. The jungle began to thin out even more, making it easier to walk. But as the day dragged on, we noticed that we were walking at a slightly upward angle. Our surroundings were changing as we continued to walk upward. Soon, we came upon an open area with large boulders that we had to go around.

"Do you hear that?" I asked David. "Yes. It sounds like screaming," he answered.

The lead warrior stopped and the head warrior walked up to him. After talking for a few moments, the head warrior spoke to the rest of the warriors. There was a short discussion, and it appeared to us that the warriors had agreed with the head warrior about something. The head warrior returned to where we were, and the entire group started walking toward the strange screaming sounds.

As we made our way around a massive bolder, we came to a large area covered with spots of dry mud and yellow grass. To the right side of this area, there was a group of fifteen to twenty monkeys. These monkeys were very different than those we had seen before. They had long narrow faces with dog-like snouts and lots of long grey hair around their heads. A few of the monkeys had brightly-colored faces. Their countenances were truly striking! Some of the monkeys' faces were bright blue on the sides with a bright red stripe that extended from their eyes to the end of their noses. The head warrior pointed to them and said, "*Nyani.*" Then he said, "*Sana mbaya*" (Very bad). His tone of voice and facial expression indicated that these animals were not to be provoked.

One large, highly-colored *nyani* charged the column, screaming with its mouth wide open, showing its incredibly long teeth. David and I stopped, but the head warrior made us continue to walk. The lead warrior banged his spear against his shield and shouted back at the charging animal. The monkey stopped and then casually yawned, revealing the longest four fangs I had ever seen, except for the great white lion.

"David, did you see the teeth on those monkeys?" I asked after we successfully passed by the troop.

"Yes, and I would not want to monkey around with any of them!" David joked.

"Stop it, David. That is not funny. Those monkeys were not only large, they were horrifying, too," I said seriously.

"I know, I know. But we are safe with the warriors and what is wrong with a little humor once in awhile?" David questioned.

I smiled, but the image of the fangs was still vivid in my mind. "You are right, David, but those strange-looking, ferocious monkeys gave me the chills."

"If you could not bond with them, Arlee, nobody could!" David exclaimed.

We both laughed. "It feels good to laugh, David. We have been in so many tough situations, and your sense of humor never fails to relieve the tension. You know, I think one of those monkeys had you in his sights!" I said, making a fierce face. We both laughed again.

As the sun began to drop closer to the horizon, the column came to a large clearing that was filled with nothing but green grass. At the far end of the clearing, David and I saw a long fence made of sticks. There was an entrance in the middle, closed by two rickety-looking stick doors. There were many cattle outside of the fence, apparently allowed to graze there during the day while a young man with a long stick tended them. His outfit was not as striking as those of the warriors, but his hair was beautifully arrayed with many colorful beads.

The head warrior looked at us, and with a proud smile, he pointed his spear at the village and said, "*Yangu nyumbani*" (My home).

David and I looked at each other, and I said, "I think he means it is their village."

"Thank goodness! I am so tired that I could sleep for a month!" David said, exhaling loudly.

"I am excited but a little nervous, David. I am wondering if his people be friendly or not. I am also thinking about what they may eat and drink? Do you think they will even accept us?" I blurted out.

"I am wondering the same and even more," David said as the column made its way to the front gate. One of the villagers opened it to let us in. The village was large, and many people had gathered around to celebrate the return of their warriors. The people stepped aside as we all entered, allowing us a path that led to the chief's hut. Many of the young girls looked at David as he walked by. They smiled, giggled, and hid their faces. Some of the young boys looked at me with quizzical expressions.

Many danced and some sang, but everyone had smiles on their faces. After we walked a distance, we approached the chief's hut. It was the largest and most highly-adorned hut in the village. The front door had been made out of an animal skin, and numerous hides were attached to the outside of the hut, as well. The hut was round in shape, and there were no windows.

As the front door of the hut was tossed aside, a large, fat man stepped out. His dark skin was complemented by the beautiful animal-skin garment that he was wearing. Holding a staff that had been decorated with brightly-colored circles from top to bottom, he moved steadfastly toward his warriors. There was much activity and celebration throughout the village, but with one loud word from the chief, everyone stopped and stared straight at him. The chief seemed very pleased to see his warriors, and then his attention turned to David and me.

He looked at David and said a few words. David could not understand him and replied, "My sister and I are from Australia and…"

The chief slammed his staff on the ground, and the head warrior stepped forward and whispered something in his ear. The great chief slowly nodded while staring at us. Then, he said some things to the entire village before sending the head warrior into his hut. In a flash, the head warrior came out with a white-skinned woman with grey hair who was clad in white cloth from her neck to the ground. She looked a bit weary, but with a big smile on her face she said, "Welcome to the *Kikuyu* tribe. My name is Alice, and this is Chief Ade."

Our mouths hung open, but no words came out. We were dumbfounded. After a long silence, I exclaimed, "You speak English!"

"Yes, my dear, I am from England. And I have been with this tribe since 1785. Where did you two come from?"

David and I looked at each other, and he finally stammered, "Ah, well, it is a long story, but we are so glad to see you. We have many questions to ask!"

"The chief has commanded a great celebration in your honor and in commemoration of the safe return of his warriors. It has been reported by the head warrior that you had a part in saving his life. We will talk later. I am sure that you would be happy to bathe and rest before the celebration. The villagers will tend to your needs." Having spoken to us, she turned around and went back inside the chief's hut.

With the head warrior standing proudly beside him, the chief thundered out instructions that were immediately followed. At once, three beautiful tribal girls appeared and surrounded me. They seemed to be about my age. One motioned me to follow them. Four young men, also about the same age as David, encircled him and motioned him to follow them in a different direction.

Most of the tribe was smiling, except for the chief and a lovely woman who stood next to him that I took to be the chief's wife. She was beautifully attired in a brightly-colored dress that was topped by a draped fabric that covered her right shoulder and chest. She had very elaborate hair adornments and was wearing many bracelets and necklaces. Above her bare feet, she was wearing several brilliantly-colored ankle bracelets. She appeared genuinely pleased to know that the warriors were safely home, but just like the chief, she acted as if there was something that was tempering her mood. It puzzled me, but without protest, both of us followed the people that the chief had assigned to us. I also wondered why Alice went back into the chief's hut so quickly.

I was led to a nearby grass-thatched hut. A flimsy door made of branches was opened, allowing me and the other girls to enter. The round hut had one large wooden pole in the middle. The walls were made of wooden poles and mud. There were no windows, and the floor was hard-packed dirt. Half of the hut was divided into three separate areas, and the other half of the hut was bare. On the left side of the entrance were four or five hammocks made of a woven, rope-like material. A small gate of sticks separated that area of the hut. The hammocks took up about a quarter of the room. They were attached to the big pole in the center of the room and to other smaller poles embedded in the wall of the hut. Next to the hammocks was an area that contained a table, a stool, and some shelving where various articles had been neatly placed. There was also a small fire pit, surrounded by rocks, about thirty centimeters away from the center pole. Looking toward the top of the center pole, I saw holes that allowed for the venting of smoke and heat. Above the center pole on the outside of the hut was a small <u>canopy</u> of sticks that was about a half meter across. It was smeared with what looked like mud. I could see that this was designed to prevent the rain from entering the vent holes. The top of the hut appeared to be made of grass that had been woven together and covered with the same muddy substance.

The final area was a much smaller room that was partitioned for privacy on both sides and had an animal hide as a door. Inside, there was a large bowl filled with water, next to which was a cup with a one-meter-long handle. The floor in the room had a mat made of thin sticks woven together by vines. Under the mat, there was a V-shaped trough in the floor that led to the outside of the hut, apparently allowing for water drainage. I assumed it was the room where the girls bathed and dressed. The hut was simple, but its design was functional.

The girls constantly talked and giggled. One of them looked at me and pointed in the direction of the room with the bowl of water in it. To my complete surprise, she said, "Do not be scared. Please be our guest in the bathing room. Push your clothes under the animal-skin door and by the time you are finished, we will have cleaned and returned your clothes."

"Oh, thank you! What is your name?" I asked in disbelief.

"My name is Hadiya. What is your name?"

"I am Arlee. How did you learn English?" I asked with great excitement.

"Miss Alice is teaching us," said Hadiya.

"Does everyone speak English here?" I asked.

"No, only a few of us, but she is determined that we will all learn."

"Please stay with me, Hadiya," I pleaded. I have never been so scared in all my life. The animals here are unbelievable. There are so many kinds, and most of them are simply fearsome."

"Yes, but you are with a good tribe. We are farmers and not a warring tribe like the *Maasai* who were chasing you. They are angry with the invading foreigners, as well as with people from their own country. I have heard that you and your brother were seen playing with the white lion. He is the most feared animal on the savanna. He often takes one of our cattle for his own. Everyone knows of him, yet you and your brother played with him. How is that possible?"

"It is a long story. Right now, I am so dirty and tired. May we talk about it later?" I asked.

"Sure! We will have your clothes back shortly," Hadiya said.

I poured the clean water over my head and down my body. It was wonderful to be able to wash the dirt and salty sweat away. I rinsed my hair as best as I could. I took my time, and when I was done, I found that one of the girls had placed my freshly washed clothes just outside the bathing room where I could reach them. My clothes had dried rapidly in the searing heat.

"We have lots of questions for you, Arlee, but we know you must rest. Sleep in one of our hammocks, and I will come for you before the celebration begins," Hadiya said with a smile. I gladly did as I was told. Gingerly, I got into one of the hammocks and was soon fast asleep.

In what seemed like an instant, I was awakened by Hadiya. It had actually been several hours, as I could see from the lowered position of the sun when we stepped outside. I did feel wonderfully rested.

"Hello, Arlee! It is time to join the celebration! Everyone

is excited about the return of our warriors and the brave thing your brother did to help save our head warrior's life," Hadiya said joyously. "I will stay with you and translate all that is said."

"Oh, thank you," I responded, looking forward to her help.

The village was bustling with life. It seemed that all of the men were sitting around talking with the children and other young men, but the women were doing all of the work of preparing for the feast. There were even women on the top of some of the huts spreading some kind of mud on the roof. The green substance was kept in a flimsy basket, and the women spread it with their hands.

As I followed Hadiya to the center of the village, I noticed that all the entrances to the villagers' huts were facing east. I realized that it made perfect sense. The sun was cooler in the morning and hotter in the afternoon.

Some of the huts had various designs on their outer walls – everything from paintings of animals to the actual hides of animals. I got the impression that the huts were an expression of the people who lived in them. The closer we walked to the center of the village, the more the huts were decorated. I noticed that the flimsy fence made of sticks and twigs was surrounding the entire village. Hadiya told me that the fence was designed to keep animals out rather than to stop warring tribes.

The center of the village was a circular area with huts surrounding it. It was about thirty meters across. The door to the chief's hut faced the circle, but strangely enough, the beautiful animal-hide door to the chief's hut remained closed.

To the left of the chief's hut was a pit where the women were preparing food for the upcoming ceremony. Some of the women were preparing food from a cow and pig that they had slaughtered and cooked, while others were pounding corn and grain to make bread in the fire pit at the center of the village. Even peas were being removed from their pods.

To the right of the chief's hut was a circular area about ten meters from one side to the other that was enclosed by a gated fence about thirty centimeters high. The rest of the circle was filled with people from the tribe.

In front of the chief's hut, animal hides had been placed on the ground and two big chairs had been placed on top of the hides. Hadiya asked me to sit down on the hides. "I will be right back," she said. As she turned to leave, David arrived in the company of one of the young men who asked him to sit down next to me on the left side of the two chairs. The young man also indicated that he would soon return.

I smiled at David and asked, "Did you have a good sleep?"

"Oh, yes! I feel human again. They let me bathe in a small stream outside the village, and it was wonderful. The only trouble was that when my translator, Azikiwe, tried to wake me, I was startled, and I fell flat on my face from the hammock!" David said, shaking his head. "How about you?"

"I slept well, thank you, and I see that you have regained your composure after the fall! But seriously, do you sense that something is wrong here in the village?" I questioned.

"What do you mean?" David asked.

"Everyone is so polite, and they always smile as they speak, but when they are not interacting with me, I sense that there is a certain sadness about them," I explained.

"You are right. I sensed that as well. It seems they are excited that their warriors are back, but something else is making it hard for them to be happy," David said quietly.

"Hadiya has been assigned as my translator, David, and I see that she and Azikiwe are returning to us." As our two helpers sat down, I said, "The smell of the food is incredible!"

David looked at Azikiwe and asked him if there was something wrong with the people. He put his head down and said he was not allowed to talk about it. Nothing else was said. Abruptly, the door to the chief's hut opened. Everyone hollered and jumped up and down. David and I immediately stood up out of respect. The chief and his wife acknowledged us as they sat in the two large chairs on the hides.

The chief slammed his beautiful staff on the ground. Everyone stopped. Not a sound was heard. Then the chief began to talk to his tribe. Our translators were ready.

"Chief Ade says that he is happy that his warriors made it home safely after their long and dangerous journey. He has been advised that his head warrior, Zuberi, was saved by you, David. He says that we all owe you our gratitude for saving Zuberi's life from the jaws of death at the river crossing. Tonight, we will have a celebration of food, wrestling, and dance to honor you. Let the fun begin!" Hadiya quietly explained to me. Azikiwe, likewise, translated Chief Ade's words for David.

At that point, Chief Ade slammed his staff down again. Everyone hollered, and a fire was lit in the large pit in the middle of the circle.

David and I sat back down and were brought a wooden plate filled with meat and vegetables, along with strange-looking goblets filled with water. Alice came out of the chief's hut and sat down next to us. She appeared to be very tired.

Looking straight at Alice, I asked, "What is wrong?" Alice nodded toward us and asked both interpreters to leave for a few minutes. Once Azikiwe and Hadiya had left, Alice explained in a soft voice that the chief's only son had been bitten by a poisonous snake and that it did not seem probable that he would live another day. The chief had no other heir, and if his son died, he would be devastated.

David and I looked at each other, and then I asked, "May we see him? I think we can help."

Alice said, "Oh, no, my dear. The chief will not allow anyone in his home except a witch doctor and me. He has had three witch doctors in, and no one has been able to help his son. He is dying."

David asked, "Exactly where is the chief's son lying in the hut?"

With a questioning look, Alice said, "He is in the chief's bed near the portion of the wall opposite the entrance to the hut." Then she said, "Do not even think about it. The chief will have you killed if you enter his home right now. I have to go back to his son's side. Your interpreters will return soon."

While we were alone, David said, "Arlee, we have to help the chief's son."

"I know. But how?" I asked.

"I have an idea."

David began to whisper in my ear. I raised my eyebrows after listening to his plan, and then I nodded in agreement. It was a risky plan, but we both agreed that we had no alternative. To sit by and do nothing was not an option, especially when we knew we might be able to help.

"The key will be getting out of our huts without being noticed," I said.

"We have to try. I will come by your hut late tonight, so be ready," David said.

"Have no worry! I will be waiting for you, David, and I will try to get some honey, too."

At this point in the festival, everyone had eaten. In the midst of their talking, dancing, and singing, the chief stood up and slammed his staff on the ground again. He said a few words and pointed to David. The entire warrior group that brought us to the village came to stand in front of us. All at once, they started jumping up and down simultaneously, just as they had done at the river bank. As they jumped, one warrior sang a phrase and the rest repeated it. It was amazing how high they jumped! While they were all dressed in the same manner, with each man having a red cloth wrapped around his chest that draped down to his shins, each warrior was wearing a different mask. All of the warriors had their necks, wrists, and ankles encircled with brightly-colored beads. Some of the warriors had painted their arms with different symbols, while others had elaborate head dressings.

David appeared to be somewhat self-conscious as the object of such attention, and he barely looked up at them, but I was captivated by their beauty and athleticism. When they finished their display of gratitude toward David, they all stopped at the exact same time and bowed. It was a moving gesture of thanks to David, and he stood up and bowed back.

The chief slammed his staff on the ground and uttered a few words to his people.

Hadiya said to us, "The chief said, 'Let the games begin!'"

"What games?" David asked.

"See that small round fence?" asked Azikiwe, pointing to the left of the circle. "Men and boys wrestle one-on-one. They use their strength to try to make their opponent's knees touch the ground. The one whose knees hit the ground first loses," Azikiwe said.

With David and Azikiwe engaged in conversation about the wrestling, I turned to Hadiya and asked, "Do you know where I can get some honey? I would be most grateful to have some."

"Sure," Hadiya replied. "I will be right back."

"Thank you!" I replied with a smile.

As I was about to tell David, two men entered the ring and shook hands. They began to circle around each other. In a flash, one man grabbed the neck of the other and pulled his head next to his. The other man also had his hands on his opponent's neck. As they struggled, each tried to pull the other down. This went on for some time before one of the men made a move that pushed his opponent off balance, causing him to land on his knees. Everyone cheered! After the winner helped his opponent up, the men bowed to one another. The winner looked into the crowd and pointed at another man.

The other man came into the ring and the wrestling started again. After several matches, the older men allowed the younger boys to play the game. The noise dramatically increased as everyone continued to offer their encouragement.

The chief and his wife remained seated in their chairs with little <u>expression</u> as they watched the games. No one looked their way, but everyone seemed determined to have a good time.

David asked Azikiwe, "Why don't they use some different moves?"

Azikiwe said, "This is all we know. What type of moves do you mean?"

Since our father had taught David how to wrestle, he asked Azikiwe, "Do both knees have to be down at the same time?"

"Yes, one knee does not count," Azikiwe replied. "Humm-m-m," David murmured.

As soon as the next match was over, Azikiwe stood up and waved to the young man in the circle and pointed to David.

"Oh, no," David exclaimed, but everyone was cheering and chanting for him to enter the circle.

David reluctantly stood up and everyone cheered even louder. He looked at Azikiwe in a way that suggested he was going to get him back for this. Azikiwe had a huge smile on his face, which made David smile, too.

"Come on, David. You can do it!" I yelled as he made his way into the circle.

David bowed to his opponent, a young man who looked to be to be of about the same age and height as David. The young man bowed, smiled, and then began to circle David in a crouched position. David did the same thing. David's opponent sprang at him, trying to get him into a headlock, but David reacted quickly and moved to one side. They continued to circle each other, staring into one another's eyes. In a flash, David lunged at his opponent with his head and shoulders straight up. Instead of grabbing his opponent's neck, David dropped to one knee and grabbed his opponent around the waist. Then, David picked him up off the ground and turned to his right, forcing his opponent to land on both knees.

There was complete silence. The young man stood up. He looked at David with astonishment but soon bowed and smiled again before leaving the circle. Everyone applauded and yelled loudly.

Soon, David was wrestling again. He dispatched everyone his age that entered the contest. Finally, one of the older men challenged him. He was a larger opponent who had been watching each match. Although David was getting tired, he realized that he must accept the challenge. The man circled David and charged with tremendous quickness, grabbing David in a headlock. The man's strength was incredible. With ease, he rose up and released his grip on David's head. Then, he bent down to one knee, picked David up, and threw him down. Both of David's knees hit the ground. It happened so fast that David was amazed at the man's speed and strength.

Everyone cheered in appreciation of the man's win. David stood up, bowed, and headed toward me. Some of the people touched his shoulder on his way back, showing their respect for his wrestling abilities.

"That man is all muscle!" David exclaimed. "He certainly learned the new move quickly!"

"You did well, my brother. I am proud of you!" I said. "Do not forget to come and get me at my hut later. It is the one with the striped hide on each side of the door. I was able to get some honey," I said, showing him the small bowl that Hadiya had placed beside me.

"That is key," David said.

"Yes. If we mix all of the melaleuca leaves from my container with the honey and saturate a long piece of string, you should be able to let the gooey mixture run down the string and onto his mouth," I answered. "The honey is in a very liquid state in this warm climate."

"Dear sister, I sure hope my plan works," David said, casting a little doubt.

"Keep our goal in focus. We both need to trust each other and put forth our best effort," I said, trying to encourage him.

"Do you think our minds are more powerful than our muscles?" David asked with a smirk on his face.

"Yes, David. With determination, we will try to accomplish something good. I believe that helping save the chief's son is the right thing to do," I concluded.

"I agree with you about doing this for the good of someone else," David said.

As the festival came to an end, David and I were courteously escorted back to our respective huts. After everyone in my hut was asleep, I stood outside, waiting for David. When he arrived, he whispered that he had watched the shafts of moonlight move three meters across the floor of his hut before leaving. None of the other young men had awakened as he carefully got out of his hammock.

As we started making our way to the chief's hut, I was carrying a long stick with a small fork at one end. When we reached the back of the chief's hut, David handed me his dagger and I carefully started <u>drilling</u> a hole about as big around as my thumb into the side of the hut, approximately one meter up from the ground. The knife was sharp, and boring the hole through the thin wall was easy. I removed the knife from the hole and looked through it into the hut.

The chief's son was exactly where Alice said he was. He was lying on his back and had been covered with beautiful animal hides. The only part of his body that was not covered was his head. His motionless face was about forty centimeters away from the wall of the hut. Everyone in the hut was asleep as a fire burned within.

I started drilling a second hole about twenty-five centimeters up from the ground at a level even with the young man's head. When it was finished, I slid the forked end of the stick through the new hole until it was right next to the young man's mouth. I notched the portion of the stick that was then at the edge of the hole to show the exact distance from the wall to his mouth. Slowly, I pulled the stick out and put it down. Next, I put all of the crushed melaleuca leaves from my container into the honey in the bowl, stirring the mixture until it was the consistency I wanted. It smelled wonderful! Then, I cut an ample length of thin twine to allow David to drop it from the roof of the hut all the way to the young man's mouth. I put the twine into the bowl filled with the mixture.

While I was doing this, David took the smaller stick that he had carried to the hut and measured the overhang of the roof by holding the stick under it. He made a notch in his stick and then laid it beside my longer stick. He made a second notch in the longer stick that indicated the combined distance from the edge of the overhang to the hole he was about to drill.

The time had come for David to start working. The question was whether or not the roof of the chief's hut would hold him. There was no turning back now. I clasped my hands in front of me to hold David's foot, giving him a boost onto the roof.

Once there, he laid across the surface and waited a few moments before starting to work. The roof held his weight without cracking or making any sounds. I held the notched stick up toward David and he grabbed it. Steadying it near the apex of the roof, he leveled the stick with both hands and pointed the notched end out toward the edge of the roof. I looked up under the edge of the overhang, and when the notch lined up with the edge, I raised my arm as a signal to David. With his dagger, he scored the spot where his end of the stick was lying. He quietly lowered the stick back down to me, and I handed the bowl up to him. Then he started to drill.

Our biggest fear had been that debris might fall from the hole onto the chief's son. We believed, however, that the fire in the room would create a small draft that would suck air toward it and up through the hole in the center of ceiling. Our hope was that the draft would be strong enough to pull the debris away from the young man's face.

After the hole was finished, David reached into the bowl and picked up the end of the twine. He started feeding it down toward the young man's head. I watched through the hole in the wall to see how close the string was getting to his face. After the twine had dropped the right distance, I waved to David. He tied the string to his thumb, and with his thumb and forefinger, he made a circle through which he carefully allowed more of the mixture to drip down the string.

Peering through the smaller hole, I was ready to address another problem that we had anticipated. The same breeze that pulled the debris away from the young man's mouth was now pulling the string. I pushed the forked end of my stick through the larger hole in the wall and was able catch the sticky string in the middle of the "V." I held the string in the proper position to ensure that the mixture found its mark. It was tedious work, but several globs landed on the young man's lips.

Suddenly, I felt a sharp object on the back of my neck. As I slowly turned my head, I saw four warriors pointing their spears directly at me. In moments, everyone sleeping near the chief's son was awake, and David was forced down from the roof. The chief was so upset that he had two large stakes placed in front of his hut. He had us tied up, hanging by our wrists. The pain was intense, but we continued to yell for Alice. She soon emerged from the hut and stood next to us.

"I told you not to try anything," she said with a look of despair. "Now the chief thinks you were trying to kill his son. What on earth were you doing?"

"We were trying to save his life!" David exclaimed as we both gasped in pain.

"Please tell the chief! We can prove it!" I shouted.

CHAPTER QUESTIONS

1. Why can the African jungle be as dangerous as the African savanna?

2. What is the mortal enemy of the king of beasts?

3. What is antivenom?

4. How does the head warrior show leadership?

5. Is overpopulation a problem in Africa?

6. Why can crocodiles and hippos live together?

7. What types of bridges can span a river?

8. How long, in feet, is the elephant's ear?

9. What is the advantage of sleeping in a hammock?

10. Are some plant species medicinal?

TRIVIA QUESTION

What animal has overpopulated the southwest coast of Africa?

CROSSWORD PUZZLES & GAMES

www.thevoyagers.net

Now that you have read the Chapter, answered the Chapter Questions, and researched the Trivia Question, it's time to go to our website! Click the PUZZLES tab and follow the directions. Remember, the underlined words in the chapter are the answers to the online CROSSWORD PUZZLE! You may want to write them down, as one of them is your CODE to play the online GAME!

HAVE FUN!

CHAPTER 4

"Let's get moving. I told Mom that we would spend a little time in the forest and then go to the tennis club to practice for tomorrow's tournament. I know she's still curious about why we go into the forest every day," Erin said.

"We had better do well in this event. If we don't, that would be a red flag for Mom and Dad," Drew replied.

"Yes, they are going to want us to justify how we are managing our time, and we can't lie," Erin said.

"Another thing is that we've been neglecting our friends lately, and that's not right. Maybe we should just tell Mom and Dad about the books at supper," Drew suggested.

"I think you're right," Erin agreed. "If we tell them what we're doing, they won't be curious or worried anymore. We can also take them to the cave and show them what we have found!"

"Okay. Let's wait and tell them after the tennis tournament. We have a few hours before we need to be at the club for our practice session, and that should give us enough time to read one chapter and get back home," Drew offered.

"Sounds good. You know, Drew, I am really relieved that we have come up with this plan. If we are up front with Mom and Dad, maybe they can help us figure out how we can practice our tennis, spend some time with our friends, and still enjoy the books," Erin concluded hopefully.

~ Book 2, Africa ~

Azizi

"I am sorry. There is nothing I can do," said Alice. "I told you not to bother the chief's son. Now Chief Ade is furious. He wants to make an example of the two of you!"

Arlee pleaded with Alice, "Please tell the chief that we only meant to help!"

Alice walked away with her head down and started to cry.

"David, this cannot be happening!" Arlee said tearfully.

"Arlee, we need to stall them. We have to give the leaf mixture time to work. I saw the chief's son licking it from his lips as I looked down through the hole in the roof of the hut!" I exclaimed.

As the sun began to rise, everyone in the village was outside watching Arlee and me <u>hanging</u> from the two poles in front of the chief's hut. There was very little talking and many of the villagers had confused looks on their faces. The chief finally appeared as he threw open the door to his hut. Everyone became silent. He walked in between us and then addressed his people. He looked up at us and shook his head. Then he walked back to his chair in front of their hut, next to where his wife was sitting. He slammed his staff down and said a few words.

Zuberi appeared with a sharp knife and walked toward us. He looked at me with despair in his eyes, then quickly looked away. He raised his knife to my throat. Just before he was about to take my life, a young man of about the same size and age as me came out of the chief's hut. He walked up to his mother and kissed her and then hugged his father, the chief.

Zuberi stopped, looked at the young man in disbelief, and then looked back at the chief. Chief Ade had his head in his hands, crying, while his wife was hugging and kissing their son.

Arlee yelled to Alice, "Please tell the chief that I can prove we saved his son's life!"

This time, Alice talked to the chief. After he thought for a moment, he said a few words to her and Zuberi.

Zuberi cut both of us down from the poles. Alice came to us and said, "Oh, my poor young friends! You have but a little time, but the chief will listen to your claim of saving his son's life."

"Alice, tell the chief that David must go to his hut and get some of our special leaves, and then I will show him how we did it," said Arlee. Alice explained to the chief what Arlee had said, and he nodded his head.

David was escorted to his hut. After securing some of the crushed leaves, he was taken back to the chief. Arlee asked Alice to translate what she was about to say to him.

"These are special leaves that we use when we are sick or have been hurt. They are what we used to save your son's life. To prove their effectiveness to you, I am asking that you slightly cut your finger and allow me to apply the leaves to your wound. You will be amazed. The pain will go away, and the wound will heal much faster than usual." The chief stared at Alice as she explained what Arlee had said.

"Do you know what you are doing?" I asked.

"Yes. Follow my lead," Arlee said with determination.

"Alright," I replied.

"David, please give me your knife," Arlee said.

"Here it is," I said.

Arlee handed my knife to the chief and showed him where to make a small cut. The chief did not seem sure about any of this, but since his son had recovered and was sitting beside him, he was willing to try it.

As blood began to run out of the chief's wound, he winced in pain. Arlee sprinkled the crushed leaves onto the chief's wound and gently rubbed them in.

The chief began to become impatient, but soon, an amazing look came over his face. He spoke excitedly to Alice, who told us that the chief's wound no longer hurt. We could all see that the <u>bleeding</u> had stopped. Alice said that the chief had never experienced anything like this before.

"We helped your son with a mixture of these leaves and honey!" Arlee said.

After Alice translated what Arlee had said, the chief stood up and looked into Arlee's eyes. As the chief hugged her, tears filled his eyes. He bowed to Arlee, and she bowed back.

The chief turned to his son and examined the spot where the snake had bitten him. The chief saw that the area looked much better. He saw that his son's face looked radiant again. Chief Ade looked back at Arlee and smiled. He grabbed his staff and slammed it on the ground. The chief's <u>decisiveness</u> on the matter was apparent as he began to address the village. Alice happily translated for Arlee and me.

"My people, it has been proven to me today how my only son was saved. Azizi, who is <u>destined</u> to take my place, escaped death because of Arlee and David. First, David saved our head warrior, and then Arlee and David saved my son's life. I declare that in five days, this village will have a feast like no other. I want you to invite our good neighbors to join us in a day of celebration for our great fortune. We will make this feast the best our country has ever witnessed. Arlee and David are our special guests, and I command that all of you treat them as our own."

The chief slammed his staff down, and everyone started yelling and dancing. Many people came to touch us, while others simply bowed. For the first time, we could see that everyone in the village was happy.

I looked at Arlee and whispered in her ear, "Father may be involved in something despicable, but at least he taught us how to use the crushed leaves to help others."

"Yes, we owe him that," Arlee agreed quietly.

"And by the way, I discovered while I was drilling into the roof of the chief's hut that the "mud" is actually sun-dried manure!"

"Apparently, it works!" Arlee whispered back with a little chuckle.

After the people had come over to show their respect, we saw Alice approaching us.

"Alice, may we have a few minutes to speak to you privately?" Arlee asked.

"Surely! Follow me. I have my own hut, and I would love to spend some time with you."

Together, we followed her to a hut that had a very beautiful animal hide for a front door. Inside, there was a table and four chairs, along with the other things that Arlee had said were in the hut where she had been staying.

"Please sit down. That was a very close call for you! Where did you get the amazing leaves?" Alice asked with a gleam in her eyes.

"First, if you don't mind, I would like to ask you a few questions," Arlee said.

"Oh, of course. I am so sorry. Please ask anything you want," Alice replied.

"Thank you. I hardly know where to begin, but my first

question is, "Where are we?" Arlee asked.

With a surprised look, Alice replied, "You are in Kenya in the shadow of Mt. Kilimanjaro. How is it that our warriors found you in the savanna?"

"We ran away from our father after we landed in Mombasa and saw evidence of slave trading. It took four days to get to your village. Now we want to get back to the port so we can find a way home," I said. "By the way, the leaves were given to us by our father."

"Home. Is that Australia?" Alice asked.

"Yes, how did you know?" Arlee questioned.

"My dear friends, I can tell by your <u>accent</u>. And also, your outfits are not from Africa. I have been here three years, and thanks to Chief Ade, I have been able to work with his tribe. When I first got here, he was unsure of me, but one of the boys in the tribe broke his finger, and with the little Swahili that I knew at the time, I convinced the chief to let me put a splint on it. As time went on, my nursing skills were respected, and Chief Ade allowed me to teach English. I believed that I could learn from these people, and I hoped that I could teach them a few things in exchange. I pray that I have done so. I know that I have learned much, and I do not regret a moment of my stay here."

"Yes, Alice, I see that your Bible is open on your table. Surely, you have been a blessing to this tribe," Arlee said sweetly.

"As you apparently observed, many white men in their ships come to the coast and take hundreds of Africans back with them to their countries and sell them as <u>slaves</u>," Alice continued. "Much of the coastal regions of Africa are at war with the white people, but they are unable to fight back because the white men have guns and cannons and the Africans have only arrows and spears. It is a tragedy, and I hope that this barbaric treatment of the African people will soon stop."

"We certainly agree," I said.

"You two are fortunate to have been found by this tribe. They have heard of what is going on, but have not yet had to experience it. If they do, then I fear they will no longer tolerate us white people," Alice stated.

"If we can get home, perhaps we can somehow convince our father that what he is doing is wrong," Arlee said softly.

"Do not worry, my dear. I will do what I can to help you get back to Mombasa. It will not be easy, and you will need to learn as much as you can about this region – the people, the animals, and the terrain. It is dangerous to travel alone, and nature operates to the extreme here.

"I heard that you saved *Eupe Kifo*," Alice said.

"Who is *Eupe Kifo*," I asked.

"He is the great white lion, the mightiest lion in Kenya. We call him "*Eupe Kifo*," which means "white death." He has the worst reputation in the country. Every month, when the moon is full, he comes here and takes one of our cattle. He is smart and cunning, and I find it hard to believe that you saved his life and that he allowed you to play with him. For years, we and other tribes have set up snares in an effort to stop him from taking our cattle. He finally stepped in one, and then you rescued him!" Alice exclaimed.

"Arlee loves animals and seems to be able to gain their trust. You should see her when we walk in the bush at home. The dingo, brumby, roo, and bitzer all follow her," I said with enthusiasm.

"Now David, are you exaggerating a bit?" Alice kidded with a grin.

We all laughed.

"You two are celebrities here, and in five days, a major festival in your honor will begin. Two nights before, the moon will be full," Alice explained.

Arlee understood the implication and said, "David, do you want to see if we can meet the lion and try to teach him to stop attacking this tribe's animals?"

"Well, bonzer. But then we need to be on our way to try and get back home," David said with a look of concern on his face.

"I agree that we must get back to the port as soon as possible. We both want to go home," Arlee complied.

Alice saw the sincerity in Arlee's eyes and heard it in David's voice. "Alright, my dear friends, I will help you in any way I can to get you back to Mombasa after the ceremony."

Arlee and I looked at each other for a moment. Then we both smiled and relaxed.

"Now, I want you to meet the chief's son, Azizi," Alice said.

We followed Alice to the front of the chief's hut, and after she knocked on the side of the hut next to the door, she said something in Swahili. Soon, the door opened, and a fine-looking young man stepped outside.

"Alice has taught me much English, and I want to thank you for saving my life. You put your lives at risk to save mine, and from this day forward, we will be brothers and sister," Azizi said with a smile and a nod.

"Azizi, it was our honor and duty to help you in any way that we could. We are grateful that everything worked out the way it did," I replied.

"I am planning to take a walk. Would you two like to come with me?" Azizi asked.

"Yes! We would love to see more of this beautiful country," Arlee responded happily.

"Please wait while I tell my parents," Azizi said.

Arlee and I heard something that sounded like arguing coming from the hut. After awhile, Azizi appeared. He seemed embarrassed. "My mother and father want me to remain within the shelter of the village in view of my recent crisis, but I convinced them that you will be accompanying me."

We looked at each other and felt uncomfortable because we knew so little about the environment. Azizi saw our hesitation and said, "Please do not worry. I am going to take you to a very safe place. My father and the other warriors have taught me many lessons in cautiousness, and I will teach you about the terrain as we travel. You are the only people with whom I have chosen to share my secret spot."

"Do you mind if I get my gear?" I asked, indicating my agreement to the plan. "I will get mine, too," Arlee said.

"I will come with you," Azizi replied.

We went from one hut to the other and were ready to follow Azizi to his special place. As we left the village, I looked back and saw Azizi's mother watching us. I could tell that she was worried about her son. Arlee and I agreed to be especially focused on our surroundings and whatever Azizi was going to teach us.

Azizi and I were walking in front of Arlee. We chatted about lots of different things. Arlee knew that we were bonding as friends and tried not to interfere. The trek was pleasant, but as we approached the mountain, the walking became harder. We stopped for awhile and looked around. The expansive view was incredible. Azizi pointed in one direction and explained the type of animals that migrated there. He then pointed in another direction and explained what was special about it. He also pointed back to the dense jungle that Arlee and I had traveled through on our way to the village. He talked about a group of people who live there that were sometimes called "Pygmies" but whose African name was "*Baka*." He said the *Baka* only live in the jungles and that they are to be feared. They try to kill anyone who crosses their part of the jungle.

"The *Baka* have been known to take people's heads and shrink them. They believe that by doing so they will be protected from intruders. Many people have gone into their part of the jungle and have never returned," Azizi said.

"Are they small people?" David asked.

"Yes. They use blow darts with a type of poison to stun their prey. Then they torture them after they wake up," Azizi stated.

"What kind of people would do that?" Arlee asked.

"We know very little about them. They seem to live underground and move from one place to another constantly," Azizi said.

Azizi took a long round object from his bag that had glass at each end. After he pulled one end of the round object, it extended in length to three times its original size. He placed the small end of the tube to his right eye and looked into it. He then scanned the savanna. After a few moments, he handed it to me.

"Where did you get that?" I questioned.

"It was given to my father by a sailor many years ago. He lets me use it when I come out here," Azizi answered. "Here, take a look!"

I took the object and looked through it just as Azizi had. It felt like I could almost touch the animals. I saw them in incredible detail.

"Arlee, you will not believe it! Look through this!" I said with excitement.

"Oh, how fabulous!" she said, peering through the glass. "This place is so beautiful. I could live here forever!"

"She loves animals," I explained, turning to Azizi.

As Arlee studied the entire savanna, she said, "I see the river, the jungle, many vines, and thousands of different animals. Africa must be the most special place in the world!"

"Arlee, we need to go soon," Azizi said.

"Oh, do we have to?" Arlee pleaded.

"Come on, Arlee. It is time to follow Azizi to his special place," I reminded her.

"Alright, alright," she said, reluctantly handing the device back to Azizi.

"We need to make up some time," Azizi said.

With Azizi in the lead, we began walking up the mountain at a faster pace. Azizi seemed to have endless energy, and my competitive spirit compelled me to stay right next to him. Arlee was beginning to fall back, however, and Azizi slowed down so she could catch up.

"It is not much further. We are almost there," he said, stopping to turn to both of us.

"What I am about to show you is a secret location. Not even my father knows of it. It would bring the white man here if others found out about it. You must promise never to tell anyone about this place. The reason I am going to show it to you is that you saved my life. Be aware that if you should tell anyone, it would destroy our village. Do you promise with your lives not to tell anyone?" Azizi asked with great concern.

"Yes!" Arlee and I each said, almost at the same time.

"No one will ever be told about your secret place by us," I exclaimed.

"I believe you. Now follow me," Azizi said.

As we began to walk between some very large rocks, Arlee asked, "Azizi, are there snakes here?"

"There are very few at this altitude, but be careful of falling rocks. Mt. Kilimanjaro is an active volcano, and at times, it will shake the whole ground," Azizi stated factually.

"A volcano? Volcanoes blow up from time to time!" I exclaimed.

"Yes, but two of the three volcanic cones are extinct," Azizi said.

"How about the third one?" I asked.

"The third is the largest, and it rumbles quite often," Azizi said.

"Oh, great! It could go at any time," I said warily.

"It is something that we live with," Azizi declared.

As we followed our new friend, there didn't appear to be any sign of a trail. After a time, Azizi slowed down and said, "What you are about to see will amaze you. For me to trust you with this secret is the highest compliment I know to give you."

"I always use extra caution as I travel the rest of the way to the cave. I take a little different route each time, in case anyone has spotted me up here. I remain low to the ground until I get to the rock that blocks the entrance to the cave. When we reach it today, I can move it more quickly if you will help me."

Arlee and I looked at each other. "A cave?" I questioned.

"Yes. The most beautiful cave you will ever see," Azizi said proudly.

Soon, the three of us easily moved the rock away from a small opening on the side of Mt. Kilimanjaro.

"Please crouch down here. I need to get something," Azizi said.

He squeezed through the small opening and came back out with a torch. Picking up two rocks, he struck them together to make a spark. When the torch was lit, Azizi instructed, "We need to pull some dry brush across the opening while we are inside."

After we helped Azizi disguise the entrance, he said, "Follow closely behind me."

We walked single file through a long passageway before coming to the main part of the cave. Azizi raised his torch up high, revealing an unbelievable sight that rendered Arlee and I speechless.

CHAPTER QUESTIONS

1. What can happen if all of the facts in a situation are not known?

2. In what part of Africa is Kenya located?

3. Would you have done what Arlee and David did to save Azizi?

4. What are the dingo, brumby, roo, and bitzer?

6. What is the main reason that slavery flourished?

7. Is there slavery today?

8. What makes Mt. Kilimanjaro unique?

9. Are there *Baka* today?

10. What country in Africa has the highest population?

TRIVIA QUESTION

How far away can a lion's roar be heard?

CROSSWORD PUZZLES & GAMES

www.thevoyagers.net
Now that you have read the Chapter, answered the Chapter Questions, and researched the Trivia Question, it's time to go to our website! Click the PUZZLES tab and follow the directions. Remember, the underlined words in the chapter are the answers to the online CROSSWORD PUZZLE! You may want to write them down, as one of them is your CODE to play the online GAME!

HAVE FUN!

CHAPTER 5

"Erin and Drew, you both did very well at the tournament today. Your mother and I are very proud of your sportsmanship," Peter said as the family was enjoying supper together.

"Thanks, Dad. You're a good instructor!" Drew said. "But we have something very important that we want to talk to you about," he added, gaining his parents' full attention. "You know that Erin and I have been going into the forest every chance we get, and we realize that it has been worrying each of you. We want to tell you that we have found something incredible."

Erin continued, saying, "To our surprise, we found a beautiful cave in the middle of the forest. It has a waterfall, stalagmites, and walls with different-colored crystals. While we were exploring it, we found a trunk in a small room behind the waterfall. It is filled with old, leather-bound books. The first volume we read was the record of an amazing adventure that took place in Europe in the year 1350 A.D. Now we're reading the second book, which is another true story about two teenage voyagers who become lost in the wilds of Africa in 1788."

"These books are fantastic! And we would like to show you and Mom what we have discovered," Drew said excitedly.

"Oh, that would be wonderful!" Peter replied. "Jean, is next Saturday good for you?"

"Certainly, dear! I can hardly wait to see this place!" Jean said enthusiastically.

"That's great, Mom. And if you don't mind, Erin and I will continue reading the second book this week while Dad is teaching at the university. I will periodically step outside the cave to see if you have called," Drew posed.

"That will be fine. Thank you for sharing this exciting news! And congratulations to both of you on a well-played tournament!" Jean said.

"Thanks so much!" Erin replied, giving her mother a kiss on the cheek. Turning to Drew, she said, "After the chores tomorrow, we'll find out what's in the cave in Kenya!"

~ Book 2, Africa ~

The Gold

David and I could not believe what we were seeing. The cave was about the size of one of the huts in the village. It was extremely warm and humid, but the amazing thing about it was that the walls were filled with shining chunks of pure gold! There was so much gold that the light from the torch made the room extremely bright. The entire back wall was completely covered in the prized metal.

"Is it not incredible, Arlee?" Azizi asked.

"This is an amazing place that certainly must be kept secret," I answered.

"Definitely," said David.

"I hate to say this, but the cave is hotter than I have ever experienced. We should not linger inside much longer," Azizi said as he went over to the right wall. With the butt of his knife, he knocked off two pieces of gold, each about the size of a baby's fist.

Azizi picked them up and handed one to me and one to David.

"What is this for?" I asked.

"This is my way of thanking you for saving my life. This is my gift to you, and you have no choice but to take it. Hide the gold in your pouches," Azizi said sincerely.

David and I both thanked Azizi as he began to lead us out of the cave. We were genuinely grateful for his gift.

Once outside, we explained to Azizi that we had come from Mombasa, and a deep frown came over his face.

"There is no way to get back to where you were except by going through the jungle where the Baka live. The river gets too wide on both the east and west side of the jungle from where you crossed, and you would even have to make a new bridge to get across it again at the narrow point. You might be better off staying here with us. After all, you are family now," he said kindly.

"We appreciate that, Azizi, but we must get home," I said gently.

"Yes, we have no choice. We will stay for the festival, but we must try to get back to the port," David said with resolution.

"I will do whatever I can to help you return there, my brother and sister, but it will be the hardest thing you have ever done. We must start now. You will need to know how to keep safe from the animals and navigate through the jungle without getting lost or hurt. I must teach you what to look out for and where to get water and food. There is much to be done," Azizi said.

"Take another look at the savanna with the telescope. I will point out some of the treasures that Kenya has, as well as some of things you need to look out for," Azizi stated.

The Voyagers Series

After we moved the rock back in front of the <u>entrance</u> to the cave, we slowly crawled away, staying low to the ground and cautiously looking in all directions.

"I always leave this place as carefully as I came in," Azizi explained as he took us in the opposite direction from which we had come. We sneaked around a number of big boulders and headed down the mountain like snakes. As Azizi stopped and looked around a large rock, to his amazement, he saw two of the warriors from his tribe.

"I might have known this would happen," he said quietly. "I know those two men, and they are not to be trusted. We need to go back to the cave and make sure we left no footprints."

The three of us made our way back to the cave's entrance and brushed away any signs that we were ever in the vicinity. We covered the entrance with rocks of many different sizes and lots of dirt and brush. Then, we started back down the mountain in the same direction that we had originally come from, covering our tracks as we walked. We were able to make it past the two warriors without them noticing us.

"Do you think they saw the cave?" I asked Azizi.

"We must hope that they did not. We will circle around them, and then let them see us walk to an outcropping of rocks. They will think we were just going to a place where we can see the savanna while sitting down," Azizi whispered.

When the warriors caught sight of us, they quickly hid themselves, thinking we had not seen them. As we reached Azizi's favorite lookout rock, the entire expanse of the savanna was visible to us.

As we sat on the rock, Azizi took out his father's telescope and began to peer through one end to find what he was looking for. He stopped and handed the telescope to me, gesturing toward some animals in the distance. I pointed the telescope in the direction he was indicating, and found three animals that seemed to be out of place on the savanna. Through the telescope, the two huge animals and one baby seemed alarmingly close. The fat animals had short, tree-trunk-sized legs. They each had two long, pointy horns on their heads, and their skin looked like sheets of metal armor. They moved surprisingly fast for their size.

Azizi said, "The *kifaru* is a dangerous animal, especially when a baby is present."

I gave the telescope to David. We were both amazed each time we looked through this wondrous invention!

"You must always stay downwind of the animals," Azizi stated. "Their ability to smell you is incredible, and if they think you are near them, they will hunt you down."

Azizi took the telescope and looked for another special animal. "A *duma* is hard to find. It is the fastest animal on the savanna," he said. After a moment, he spotted a mother and three cubs.

"Look right over there," he said, handing the telescope back to me.

Just as I spotted them, the mother suddenly took off running after a small deer. Her speed was incredible, and the cat's ability to make sudden changes in direction seemed impossible. In a few seconds, the mother cat caught her prey. I gave the telescope to David. He had not seen the *duma* run, but he saw how she killed her prey with a strong bite to the neck.

"The *duma* is one animal that will not hunt you," Azizi stated as he spotted a different group of animals.

He pointed in the opposite direction and said, "That is a *simba*, one of the most dangerous animals on the savanna. They hunt in packs, and once they target an animal, they split up and set a trap for it. You must stay away from these animals. The male *simba* has a huge, hairy mane. Although he is much bigger and stronger than the females, he is lazy, except that he will fiercely protect his pride."

Azizi changed the subject quickly as he looked at us intently. "Is it true that you were both playing with *Eupe Kifo* when our tribesmen found you?"

"When we came upon the great white lion, he was dying. We removed the snare and used our special leaves to save him. He seemed to understand that we helped him, and he let us play with him. I was never so scared in my life!" David explained.

"Where did the leaves come from?" Azizi asked.

"Our father gave us the leaves and showed us how to use them. He never let us go anywhere without them," Arlee said softly.

"Your father must be a wise man," Azizi said.

David and I looked at each, guessing that we were both probably thinking, *If he is so wise, why would he be selling good men for slaves?* Neither of us said anything to Azizi.

"I must show you many other things," Azizi explained. "It is best not to go to high places, like rock mounds, on the savanna. Cats use those places to survey the land for prey, and snakes live in many of the crevices in the rocks."

Azizi pointed the telescope toward the jungle. "The jungle may be the most dangerous place here in Kenya. It has poisonous snakes, spiders, ants, <u>insects</u>, and scorpions. There are boa constrictors that can eat you whole, cats that pounce from trees, bats that will suck your blood, and elephants that can trample you, just to name a few of its residents. You will need to be especially careful in the jungle," he said as he handed the telescope to David.

David viewed the huge mass of trees that they would have to make their way through before getting to the savanna. He looked from one end to the other, knowing that we had no choice but to cross somewhere near where we crossed before. He looked down as handed the telescope to me.

"What is wrong, David?" I asked.

"The jungle has me worried, Arlee. We must learn as much as possible before we go next week," he replied.

Azizi continued to point out many different animals and

tried to educate us on each one before finally saying, "It is getting late. We should get back to the village."

As we stood up and began down the mountain, Azizi looked behind us several times. When he saw one of the warriors dart behind a rock, he was still worried that his secret cave may have been discovered.

With the sun beginning to slip over the edge of the savanna, the sky turned beautiful shades of orange and yellow. There was not a cloud anywhere to be seen. It seemed so peaceful, but David and I knew that it was time for the predators to wake up. Beauty and horror characterized the savanna at night.

When we entered the village, Azizi bid us a good night and went to his family's hut. David and I found a place to sit and talk before going to our huts.

"David, while we were up on the mountain, I had a profound realization. It was about the way I think about the past, today, and the future. I have been very stressed over our current situation, but when we were looking over the savanna with Azizi, it came to me that I must concentrate on what I am doing now and not allow myself to think of 'what was' or 'what if.' Do you understand?" I asked.

"I think so, Arlee, but how can just thinking about today help you or me?"

"It is more than just thinking about today," I answered. "It is refusing to let something that we have no control over paralyze us."

"Yes, and that should allow us to remain more alert to the things around us. If we can control our fear, we should be able to make better choices," David said.

"We will have a lot of choices to make, for sure, but right now, we need to get some sleep," I said.

"See you in the morning," David replied.

I went into my shared hut and put my things under the hammock, keeping only the leather bag that contained the gold next to my side.

In the morning, I found David waiting for me a short distance from my hut. We walked around and saw a busy village at work. When Azizi saw us, he hugged me and nodded respectfully to David.

"I would like to get your advice about *Eupe Kifo*," Azizi said.

"Certainly," I said. "What would you like to know?"

"Follow me, please," Azizi answered.

We walked to the stream next to the village and sat on the grass. When we were certain that we were alone, Azizi started to talk.

"Every full moon, we lose one of our cows to *Eupe Kifo*. We have tried almost everything to stop him, but he is cunning and powerful. We have enclosed the cows in a fenced area, but he sneaks up and <u>stampedes</u> the cows, making them leave the safety of the fence. We have placed many snares to capture him, but after years of trying, we have had no success. He will come again in three nights under the full moon to take one of our cows. Yet he played with you after you saved his life. Do you have any idea as to how we might stop him from taking our cattle?" Azizi asked with great sincerity.

I looked at David. We were both quiet for many moments.

Finally, I said, "We spoke to Alice about this, and we would like to try to meet with the great cat."

"This cat is the largest, meanest, and most skillful animal on the savanna," Azizi said sternly. "He can kill with one swipe of his paw. I am not asking you to risk your lives. He is not to be taken lightly, and I, for one, do not want to see either of you hurt."

"We are not afraid of the cat. We feel strongly that we

bonded together in some inexplicable way when we saved his life. My brother and I are willing to see if we can communicate on some level with the cat to let him know that your cows are off limits to him. We must have your word that you will not tell anyone. I also want you to come with us," I said with great <u>conviction</u>.

"You just saved my life. Do you now want me to be eaten by *Eupe Kifo*?" Azizi asked in amazement.

"I must ask you to trust me one more time. If he meets you as our friend and knows that you live here, then he will stay away. But if he does not know you and sees our departure, he might come back after we have gone."

"Well, I see your point. But, I will stand behind you, quite a good distance behind you," Azizi said sheepishly.

There was a long silence. Then Azizi added, "Today, I think we should go up to the cave and see if those two men found it. Will you join me after our midday meal?"

"Absolutely!" David said. "After we check on the security of the cave, we would like to go back to your favorite rock so you can show us more animals."

"Count me in, too," I said happily.

The chief, his wife, Azizi, Alice, David and myself shared a simple but filling meal of various fruits, figs, hot round bread, milk, and water. We all enjoyed the time together, with Alice and Azizi translating for us.

As we finished, Azizi respectfully addressed his parents. "Arlee, David, and I are going to my favorite rock on the mountain. I will show them more of our home and explain the many wonders that Kenya has to offer before they begin their journey back to Mombasa."

The chief wished us well and said to be back before dark.

As Azizi, David, and I began our climb, we were careful

to check and see if anyone was following us. Convinced that we were alone, we talked about many things along the way.

We maneuvered around the many large rocks by taking a different route than we had the first time, but when we finally reached the entrance to the cave, we were stunned to see that there were footprints everywhere.

"I knew it!" Azizi said furiously.

"Azizi, please calm down! Being upset will not allow you to think clearly, and right now, we need you to think about what to do next," I said.

"I will kill those men!" Azizi said with a vengeance.

"No, Azizi! Please listen to me! There is too much killing in this world. If you kill them, you are no better than others that kill. We must find a better way," I said.

Suddenly, the entire mountain began to shake. The rumbling went on for quite some time, but just as abruptly as it had started, it stopped.

"Mt. Kilimanjaro is waking up!" David said with fear.

"It started this about six months ago," Azizi said, still seemingly more concerned about the men who had found the cave.

As David and I looked up, we saw a small cloud of smoke rising from the top of the mountain. It drifted in the opposite direction of the village.

Azizi was still staring at the entrance to the cave. "We must pile up as many big rocks as we can. It is about all we can do at the moment," he said.

Despite what had happened at the cave, Azizi led us to favorite rock once again. He took out his telescope and looked toward the river, keeping his promise to continue teaching us the things we needed to know.

Handing the telescope to David he said, "Look in the river over there. You will see a large fat animal. The _kiboko_ is the worst offender when it comes to killing humans. They have killed more of us than any other animal. Although the _kiboko_ is big and rounded, it can run surprisingly fast, and if you happen to come upon one that has a baby, it will pursue you with the intent to kill. You must stay away from these animals."

"Do all of the countries in Africa have the _kiboko_? David asked.

"The _kiboko_ lives in many countries in Africa, but primarily it lives where there is a good supply of water," Azizi answered. "Alice has taught us that there are many countries in Africa and that Africa is one of the largest continents in the world."

"Can you name all seven of the continents?" David asked Azizi.

"Oh, yes, of course. They are Asia, Australia, North America, South America, Europe, Africa, and Antarctica," he said with confidence.

"You have learned much from Alice," David said.

"Yes, we ask her about many things, and she informs us of many things that we would not even know to ask about!" Azizi said. "She is very kind in teaching us."

As David and Azizi were talking, I was looking through the telescope. "Look at that beautiful spotted cat! It walks so confidently and gracefully," I exclaimed.

"The *chui* is more afraid of you than you are of him, but he can be dangerous if you back him up into a corner. Did you know that the only cat family that lives together and works as a group is that of the *simba*? I know *Eupe Kifo* has a pride somewhere, and that is one pride I would stay away from. Prides work together to kill animals many times their size. When they eat, the males go first, then the females, and finally, the young. They are vicious, even when they eat. It is a good thing that they sleep sixteen to twenty hours a day! The male also marks his territory, and if another male crosses it, they go to war. If the invading male wins, he kills all of the cubs in the pride. The new cubs will come from him," Azizi explained.

I listened to every word and became even more intrigued with Kenya and its animals. David thanked Azizi for teaching us so many things and said that we would be mindful of these facts as we made our way back to Mombasa. We all avoided discussing the possibilities regarding the cave.

Abruptly, another large rumble from the mountain shook the ground. "This is the most activity I have experienced in my life," Azizi admitted with surprise. "We had better return to the village."

As we made our way down the mountain, we all looked back and saw another column of smoke spewing from the top. When we got to the village, there were worried looks on everyone's faces. Azizi was told that his father was considering moving the village because the mountain was angry. The older tribesmen were apparently telling stories that they had heard from their grandparents about the volcano erupting during their ancestors lives.

On our way to Azizi's hut, there was a deafening blast and the mountain spewed skyward! The ground shook violently, and everyone stopped and looked up at the summit. A small river of lava began to flow down the side of the mountain toward the village as tremors continued to be felt beneath our feet. Then, as quickly as it began, the shaking stopped. We saw that the smoke was being taken by the wind in the opposite direction of the village. The lava flow that was visible to us stopped part way down the mountain, and the village was spared. The majority of the lava that we had seen fly into the air had apparently flowed down the opposite side of the mountain.

"Well, that was fun!" David said with a smile.

"We could have been killed, and you are making us laugh," I said, shaking my head but grinning at the same time.

"What is the point of thinking negatively?" David asked.

"Please explain what that means," Azizi said.

"Certainly. The way I see it, I am in control of my thinking and my mood. I can evaluate what other people say and do, I can observe what happens in nature, but I reserve the right to decide how all of it will affect my attitude. I know that each day is precious, and that I am solely responsible for my thoughts and actions during every one of them. There is so much to learn! So, I want to have the courage to make personal decisions that reflect good character and a positive outlook. If I think negatively and always expect the worst, it would be impossible to be a source of encouragement to anybody! I want to respect both the environment and other people, and the bottom line is that I want to avoid making decisions that will cause me to be regretful," David said in complete seriousness.

Azizi remained silent, so I spoke first. "You certainly have learned a lot, David, and I agree with you wholeheartedly!"

The mountain was silent and no more smoke appeared

at the top. Azizi looked up at the volcano and then at David. He said, "For the first time, I have seen how big this mountain is and how small I am in relation to it and everything else around me. I am going to remember what you have said, David. I will let your wisdom guide me in the future. I know that there will come a day when my decisions will affect the whole village." Azizi paused and then said, "Will you both come with me to check the cave tomorrow?"

"As long as this mountain does not blow its top again!" David exclaimed. We all enjoyed a good laugh.

That night, David and I were invited to the chief's hut to have dinner and talk. It was a great honor, and we appreciated it. When we entered the chief's hut, we bowed to the chief and his wife. Alice was also there, along with Azizi. We sat in a circle on top of many beautiful animal hides that covered the floor. I noticed that there were highly decorative tapestries and rugs hanging from the walls. I also saw various shields, spears, and knives.

"Why did you come to Kenya, Alice?" I asked.

"It is a long story, but I will keep it short. I did much research before I came. I looked at the maps, studied the culture, and read about the simple life that this tribe leads. The latter is what intrigued me. They never destroy the land or take more than they need to eat. They share all that they have. They pass down their heritage and culture from generation to generation. In Africa, the family unit is extremely important. All of this pleased me. So here I am, under the care of Chief Ade, who was kind enough to accept me, even though I was a stranger."

With Alice translating what was being said for the chief and his wife, the couple seemed to be enjoying the conversation.

"Azizi, tell us how you learned so much about the animals," I said.

"We are taught from childhood about all of the animals, their habits, their territories, and what to be wary of. The animals and jungles of Africa are our greatest assets, and we <u>protect</u> them with our lives. During one brief lapse in judgment, I got bitten by the snake. I should have known better. That will not happen again. The rules in the wild are not bent for anyone. The animals have their own code of life and each person must learn that code to survive. I will do my best to teach you as much as I can in the short amount of time we have together. My father knows about all of the animals and their habits, but he has yet to learn English. However, we have a fine, patient teacher here!" Azizi said, nodding at Alice.

"I know I would enjoy living here, Azizi," I said. "I love animals so much that I would be right in my element!"

"Forgive my sister, but there are times that I think she is part animal!" David said, nudging me with his elbow.

As we all laughed, people began to come in and out of the chief's hut with various foods and drinks. It was such a special time for us. We talked for a long time and, as always, I wanted to learn more about the animals, and David was more interested in how to get back to the port.

When the evening came to a close, David and I went to our respective huts for a good night's rest before heading for the cave in the morning.

Not long after dawn, I emerged from my hut to find Azizi and David chatting quietly outside. I gave each of them a hug, and the first thing that David said to me was that he had fallen out of his hammock again! After Azizi checked to see that we all had the necessary gear, we began our walk toward the base of the mountain.

We followed the same trail up the mountain that we used before the eruption, and even though the trail seemed familiar to David and I, there were definitely some differences. We had to walk around a very large rock that was not there before. The higher we went, the more changes we noticed. At one point, the trail disappeared, yet further up, we came to it again. New rocks and boulders were strewn here and there, but the trail still led up to the cave.

No one talked as we climbed because everyone was worried about what we might find. As we got closer to the area, we saw that lava had spilled from the top of the mountain down to the level of the cave. We could not get too close because the lava was still hot, but we could see that the lava had permanently sealed the entrance!

"The cave is gone! There is no trace of the entrance, and lava is everywhere!" Azizi exclaimed.

David and I took out the chunks of gold that Azizi had given us and attempted to hand them back to him.

"What are you doing?" Azizi questioned. "The gold is my gift to you. I have been coming to this cave for years, and I took chunks out every time I came. The gold is hidden all around our territory, and if our tribe ever needs help, I will retrieve some of it as necessary. The best thing about this is that the cave is impenetrable. Those men who followed us here will never be able to get at the gold," Azizi said with relief.

Perhaps the largest burden of Azizi's young life had been lifted. David and I knew that if the cave had still been accessible, it would have brought misery to Azizi's tribe. Men would have killed to get to the treasure.

Amid hugs and smiles, Azizi led us to his favorite perch on the mountain where we talked more about the animals of Kenya and human survival amongst them.

Azizi spoke for a long time and pointed out many different animals and birds. He explained the habits of each and what to be mindful of. He talked about the hidden reptiles and insects. The more he explained, the more I understood that there were three basic traits that the animals had in common. First, they were unpredictable. Second, they had either a keen sense of smell, hearing, or eyesight. And third, they preferred to stay away from humans.

Turning to Azizi, I said, "During the night of the full moon, we will try to meet *Eupe Kifo*. David and I will stand in front of you and try to re-connect with him. I believe Eupe Kifo will remember us and that our friendship will influence his behavior," I said with conviction.

"I sure hope so, Arlee. That cat is huge," David said.

"He is the largest and the most ferocious of the male lions in Kenya. He has been known to take a buffalo down by himself," Azizi said.

Azizi seemed bewildered at the prospect of encountering *Eupe Kifo*, and David had a few reservations, but I was supremely confident.

"We had better start heading back. It is getting dark, and I am sure that our meal is waiting," Azizi said.

On the way back to the village, little was said. Each of was probably absorbed in thoughts about meeting the cat. When we returned, David and I were invited to eat with the chief's family again.

Azizi continued to freely share his knowledge with us. His family had taught him well. After the meal, we thanked the chief and headed back to our huts. On the way, David suddenly stopped walking and asked, "Do you think it is a good idea to take Azizi with us? What if something goes wrong? We would really be in trouble."

"You just may be right, David. I know we can do this, but after listening to Azizi explain how unpredictable wild animals are, we cannot expect him to get involved. Do you want to go back to the chief's hut and ask Azizi to come outside so we can to explain the situation to him?" I asked.

"Arlee, I think I should be the one to tell him. I will talk to him tomorrow," David decided.

"Alright, my brother. Maybe 'man to man' is better in this situation. Good night, David. I will see you in the morning," I said, feeling better about the whole matter.

The morning came quickly, and the day went by too fast. Azizi taught us even more about the animals, the jungle, and the savanna from his favorite vantage point. On the way back down the mountain, David explained to Azizi that both of us would feel better if he would stay in his hut when we met the cat. Azizi started to argue, but he realized that David was determined to avoid threatening the safety of the chief's only son.

"Please remember to keep our plan a secret," David said.

"I will," Azizi said.

The evening was one of laughter and great food. After David and I left the chief's hut, we sat by the stream to discuss our plans to meet the king of beasts.

CHAPTER QUESTIONS

1. What are the *simba*, *chui*, *kifaru*, *kiboko*, and *duma*?

2. Why do some animals in the African savanna migrate?

3. Why don't all of the animals on the African savanna migrate?

4. What is the fastest animal in Africa?

5. What cat is larger than a male lion?

6. What makes African lions unique?

7. Why is it important to preserve African jungles and

savannas?

8. What wild animal scares you the most?

9. If you were Azizi, would you have shown Arlee and David the cave?

10. Are you able to keep a secret?

TRIVIA QUESTION

How many gallons of water can an adult elephant drink in a day?

CROSSWORD PUZZLES & GAMES

www.thevoyagers.net
Now that you have read the Chapter, answered the Chapter Questions, and researched the Trivia Question, it's time to go to our website! Click the PUZZLES tab and follow the directions. Remember, the underlined words in the chapter are the answers to the online CROSSWORD PUZZLE! You may want to write them down, as one of them is your CODE to play the online GAME!

HAVE FUN!

CHAPTER 6

"Before you start reading, Drew, I want you to know that I've been thinking a lot about the preservation of the cave and these books," Erin said.

"You and me both. Let me guess! You were thinking about how we haven't used any caution while coming into the cave or leaving it," Drew suggested.

"Exactly! I think we need to read just one more chapter today and then carefully leave the cave and wait for Mom and Dad to come with us this weekend. Maybe Dad will have some ideas as to how we can protect this place," Erin said.

"Yes. We both know what an expert he is in preserving the many costumes in his collection. This should be of great interest to him," Drew said, filled with anticipation.

~ Book 2, Africa ~

The Son

I woke up first and headed toward Arlee's hut. There was a slight breeze coming down from the mountain, and the moon was almost straight up in the sky. The air temperature was cool and the village was silent. As I approached the hut, Arlee crept through the opening. We quietly made our way to the edge of the village where the cattle were still penned in, awaiting the villager who would let them out to the grassy area to graze.

"Are you sure about this?" I asked.

"Yes, David," Arlee replied confidently. "Remember what we need to do? He has to smell us first."

Arlee licked her finger and lifted it over her head to determine the direction from which the wind was coming. She knew the lion would come from the opposite direction, so the wind would blow his smell away from the cattle and they would not be able to detect his approach. Arlee led me downwind of the cattle, so the lion would smell us first.

As we waited, the cattle seemed to be at ease. The moon moved ever so slowly as it glided to the top of the sky. I started to get impatient, and as I was about to say something to Arlee, a few of the cattle began to make some sounds.

Arlee and I both stared into the darkness but saw nothing. We remained fully alert as the cattle became more and more restless. The moon was shining so brightly that shadows of the trees and bushes were being cast on the ground.

Suddenly, we heard a low growl. I grabbed Arlee's hand as we both stared straight ahead. None other than Eupe Kifo casually walked up to us and flopped down on the ground. Arlee cried for joy, but I stood there like a statue with a fixed expression.

The great king of beasts had remembered both of us and wanted to play! He had gained a lot of weight back since we last saw him, and his white hair and thick mane were gorgeous. It was easy to see how he was able take down animals twice his size. Arlee hugged his massive head and kissed the side of his face. I finally dropped to my knees and scratched his back. The three of us rolled around happily, and for the briefest of moments, Arlee and I forget all else. It was absolutely thrilling.

All of a sudden, the white lion jumped up, put his ears back, and started growling. His strength and quickness were unbelievable. He was staring at something, and when Arlee and I got to our feet, we saw what he was looking at. About thirty meters away, there stood Azizi, awestruck. Arlee quickly stepped in front of the lion, put her hands on her hips, and loudly said, "No!" She pointed her right index finger to the ground in front of the cat and said, "Stay!" Then, she turned and walked to Azizi.

I stood next to the cat, stroking his mane with both hands. The cat stopped growling and perked up his ears as he watched Arlee go over to Azizi.

"What are you doing here, Azizi? You look like you are about to faint!" Arlee exclaimed. Azizi did not answer. He just stared at the cat with his mouth open.

"Are you alright?" Arlee said a little louder.

Azizi slowly turned his head toward Arlee and said, "I had to come. I had to see for myself."

"Are you alone?" Arlee asked.

"Yes," Azizi replied.

"I want you to come with me, Azizi, and do exactly as I say," Arlee said. "As we approach the cat, do not look straight into his eyes. Put the back of your right hand out slowly toward his nose."

Arlee and Azizi walked together toward the attentive cat. As the cat's ears started to flatten backward, Arlee said, "No!" She hugged Azizi, and immediately, the lion's ears went up. I told Arlee that I felt his muscles relax. Azizi slowly extended the back of his hand toward the cat's nose. The lion sniffed Azizi's hand, and then looked at Arlee. After Arlee hugged Azizi again, the lion licked Azizi's hand. The look on Azizi's face was priceless!

"Now, pet his head," Arlee told Azizi. The great lion allowed Azizi to pet him, and before long, the cat laid down, inviting all three of us to play.

We spent a long time giving the animal all the love we had. Finally, Arlee stood up and asked Azizi and I to stand next to her. The big cat remained sprawled on the ground, yawning.

"I think we should call him 'Zar,'" Arlee stated. "That would be spelled, 'Z-A-R.' I know that the word 'czar' means 'emperor,' so I am just spelling it a little differently," Arlee explained.

"I like it," Azizi said.

"It is perfect," I agreed.

Arlee bent down in front of the lion, looked him straight in the eyes, and said, "Zar." She pointed at him and again said, "Zar." Then she hugged him and said, "Zar, I love you!" With that, the great beast was given the name of Zar. Azizi and I joined Arlee in playing with Zar, calling his new name over and over again. Soon, the big cat seemed to understand his new name and looked in the direction of the person who was saying it.

"Azizi, I think it is important that no one else knows that

we are friends with Zar. You should be the only one who ever says his name, and I do not recommend that you play with him. He will know it is you when you call his name. Be sure to stand downwind so he can smell your scent. You must also protect Zar from your people. I do not believe they would understand the cohesive bond that we have and would still try to kill him. Now, I want the three of us to stand in front of the pen where the cattle are," Arlee directed.

As we got up and moved over to the pen, Zar stayed put, looking like a monster kitten on the ground. Arlee stood between us, and with our backs to the cattle, she called, "Zar, Zar!"

Zar looked up at Arlee. She pointed at the cattle and said in a stern voice, "No!"

Zar stood up and slowly walked over to Arlee. Arlee looked into his eyes, and again pointed at the cattle in the pen and said, "No!"

It was one of the most incredible things Azizi had ever experienced. His eyes watered in amazement.

Zar kept looking at Arlee as he moved his massive head to one side and then the other. He sat down, and Arlee hugged him. He licked her right cheek with his extremely rough tongue, leaving some unique scratches of love and respect on her face!

The three of us completely lost track of time as we played with Zar. For whatever reason, Zar decided that it was time for him to leave. He rose up, looked at us, and then headed off into the jungle. Arlee, Azizi, and I stood and watched, unable to utter a word. We could hardly believe the experience that we had just had.

Finally, Azizi said, "I am so grateful to be alive and to have made the decision to come here today. I am forever indebted to you for two great things – enabling me to survive the snake bite and introducing me to Zar!"

Knowing that we could not possibly get to sleep after what

had happened, we decided to sit outside the pen and talk for awhile.

Arlee was her analytical self. She reviewed every moment of the night again and again. She wanted to understand Zar's every movement in order to better communicate with him. She also realized that while she had a special relationship with this particular lion, she should stay away from all other lions.

I kept thinking how small and insignificant I was next to Zar. I continued to be amazed at his strength, power, and speed. I thought how futile it would be to try to run away if he was <u>chasing</u> me. I had never been next to such a large and powerful animal.

Azizi freely poured out his emotions. He said that Arlee and I had taught him how to better communicate and that if he took his father's place in the future, he would rule with compassion and humility. He said that he wanted very much to help us get through the jungle. He mentioned that he had some other ideas, but he did not elaborate.

As dawn approached, we walked back toward the huts, still discussing our interaction with Zar. Realizing that we were getting within earshot, I said, "We had better stop talking about this so no one will hear us. This must remain our secret!" Arlee and Azizi agreed.

It was an especially gorgeous morning. The sun glowed brilliantly in a cloudless sky. A fresh breeze was blowing, and as it filtered through the jungle leaves, it carried with it a wonderful, clean smell, accented by the aroma of sweet flowers. Arlee told me that she wanted to learn more about what the women of the tribe did, so she found her interpreter. They chatted incessantly as they waved to me and walked toward the area where several of the women were already assembled. Arlee had seemed particularly interested in learning how the women made beautiful jewelry out of so many different items that had been highly <u>polished</u>.

Azizi told me that he was going to put together a group of young men to go hunting for the evening meal. I gladly accepted his invitation to join them.

There were four other young men with us. Azizi said something to them in Swahili and we started walking, forming a single file. As we went out through the village gate, I was next to last in line, with Azizi behind me. We were heading south, the direction from which Arlee and I had initially come into the village.

"David, we are going to hunt for one monkey and one deer. As you know, we love all animals, so we only take what we need to survive. These two types of animal are plentiful, and with our fruits, breads, and vegetables, they will feed the entire tribe. Do you want to watch or would you like to try to get one of them yourself?" Azizi asked.

I thought for a moment and said, "I would like to try myself, but what do you mean by 'get one'?"

"We use darts," Azizi said.

"Oh, yes. Zuberi let me try his blowgun on our way to the village," I said.

"We each have one," Azizi said. "The darts are treated with a poison, and after we hit our target, we wait until the animal is dead. We sometimes have to use two or even three darts to bring down bigger game, but one is usually enough for a monkey."

The blowguns were all beautifully carved and painted, with each one being unique. Every young man wore a leather sack at the waist that contained the poisoned darts.

"Where do you get the poison for the darts?" I asked.

"The poison that we use comes from the frogs we find in the jungle. These frogs are plentiful, but we do not kill them," Azizi explained. "We just rub the tip of the darts on their backs where a sticky, poisonous substance is found. The frogs are easy to locate because they are brightly colored. Some are black with bright yellow spots, while others have bright green stripes. I guess it is nature's way of telling would-be predators to watch out!"

"It was certainly made plain to me not to touch the poisoned end of the dart on our way to your village!" I recalled.

"As I have explained before, the jungle is full of poisonous creatures," Azizi continued. "That is why we walk in a single file, with the front man using a long stick that he swipes back and forth on the ground in front of him. We must have the greatest respect for the power of the jungle."

Along the way, there was some idle chatter amongst the men that I did not understand, but I was focused on everything around me. The jungle was still a distance away, and dry, knee-high grass covered the surrounding land, with various trees interspersed. Soon the trees became thicker, and Azizi said, "We need to be careful now because we are coming upon a large family of baboons. It is alright if they see us, but we do not want to provoke them in any way. The males are big and fast. They will defend their families to the death with their large teeth." I remembered the terror that I had experienced along this part of the trail, but as we wove our way through the big boulders, our column passed by the baboons without incident this time.

Azizi continued to catch me looking back at Mt. Kilimanjaro. "Did you know that Mt. Kilimanjaro is the largest and tallest single <u>mountain</u> on earth and that it is made up of three separate volcanoes?" Azizi asked.

"I did not. When you took us up to your favorite place in the foothills, we were only high enough to see the savanna, but as we move further away from the mountain, we get quite a different perspective. I have so much to learn about your land, and I really wonder if I will be able to successfully lead Arlee back to Mombasa," I said with frustration.

Azizi came over and put his arm around my shoulder. "I have been told that we are learning something new every day and that we never stop learning until we die. You know many things that I do not, and there are things I know that you do not. Together, we are becoming more informed by listening to one another. I have a feeling you will learn more about this world we live in than I will ever know," Azizi said kindly.

"Thanks, Azizi. Your generosity has been incredible, and I wish we did not have to leave you, but we must return home. You will always be my best friend," I said with a smile.

I saw that the dense jungle began about five hundred meters away from where we were. It seemed odd to me that there was such a sharp dividing line between the jungle and the savanna. It was here that the leader took out a three-meter-long stick and began sweeping it along the ground from side to side in front of him.

I was made aware once again of the very different environment in the jungle – the air, the sounds, the light, the smell, and even the temperature. I recalled how vivid these distinctions were on our initial journey to the village. Two of the young men in the column were now looking up into the trees, while the other three were looking around the floor of the jungle. I mimicked their manner of walking much more carefully so as not to make any noise. I sensed that the column had gone into a hunting mode.

Soon, we began to hear loud hooting noises. When we got closer to the sound, the leader stopped the column. Azizi came to my side and pointed to the left, up into the canopy of trees. "See it?" he whispered.

I looked everywhere but saw nothing but branches and leaves. Azizi smiled and stood in front of me, saying, "Watch where my finger is pointing."

I squinted and looked where Azizi was indicating. Then I saw a large black monkey sitting on a branch, looking right back at me. I was amazed that the rest of the men easily saw the monkey, but I had to be shown. I realized that I needed to become much more aware of the things around me if Arlee and I were going to make it back to the port.

Azizi carefully took out a dart from his leather pouch and put it into the end of the blowgun. As he handed it to me, he said, "Rest the blowgun on my shoulder and try to hit our prey." I rested the far end of the long device on Azizi's shoulder, took a deep breath, and aimed. When I thought my aim was true, I blew as hard as I could into the blowgun. The deadly missile flew silently through the air toward its victim.

The monkey howled and jumped off the branch. My dart was close, but it hit the branch that the monkey was sitting on and not the monkey itself. If I had aimed a little higher, I would have hit the monkey. I had not allowed for the fact that gravity had caused the dart to fall as it flew toward its target. I would not have impressed Zuberi and his warriors with this attempt!

"I am sorry to have lost one of your darts, Azizi," I said.

"Do not worry, my friend, they are easy to make," Azizi assured. "Your first shot was close. I think you will master this quickly."

I was determined to watch the young men in the column in order to pick up some new techniques in jungle surveillance. I saw that they already had considerable experience in detecting various types of animals.

"Azizi, what factors are important as you seek a target?" I asked.

"There are three basic things that we focus on. One is

sound, two is unusual color difference, and three is movement. This is easier for us in places we have been before, since we know the foliage, the habits of the animals, and their migration routes. We never take a baby away from its mother, and we make sure there are many of the same kind of animal before we take it. We never kill for sport, only for food. We also use every part of the animal. We respect the animals and never underestimate them. This is their home, too, and we believe that we must take care of them," Azizi explained.

The leader stopped again. This time, I saw the animal. It looked like a large deer, and it had not noticed us. Two of the young men aimed their blowguns at the animal, and in a flash, both darts found their mark. The deer was stunned and tried to pull the darts out with its teeth, but it quickly succumbed and fell to the ground.

After hearing the sound of another monkey, two of the remaining men took off into the jungle. Azizi and the first two men made their way to the fallen deer. I watched as one of the men found a thick branch that was about two meters long. The men cut the twigs off the branch to make it smooth. Using some dry grass rope that they had been carrying, they tied the legs of the deer to the branch. Each of the two men put one end of the branch on his left shoulder, and they began walking back the way we came.

The other two men who had run into the jungle soon caught up with our group. They were carrying a large black monkey that was also tied to a thick branch. I was impressed with how these people used the jungle so efficiently to care of their tribe. There was no waste of time or bounty.

"The tail bones of this monkey will make good jewelry pieces as will the back bones of both of the animals," Azizi explained. "Every man here will receive an article of jewelry from each of these animals. The elderly men of the village prepare these pieces for the women to assemble. In this way, we commemorate these animals," he continued.

I was astonished at the way Azizi and his tribe thought of the animals. They paid tribute to the ones they had to take for food. It was apparently a belief that had long existed. They cared more about the animals than I had imagined, and they knew more about the animals' habits than any other people I had ever met.

As we left the jungle and began walking in the savanna, the leader stopped and made a sign for everyone to get down. A pride of lions was crossing in front of us. In view of their close proximity, it was a distinct advantage that our group was downwind of the lions, because if they had smelled us and our cargo, they would have attacked, if only to get the fresh deer and monkey meat.

"Lions are opportunists," Azizi whispered. "While they often ambush live animals, they will also scavenge for food. There are only three kinds of animals that will challenge a lion. One is the elephant, and he just wants the lions to move away from the path he is walking on. The second is the hyena, which is the mortal enemy of the lion, but only in large packs. Hyenas are afraid of the male lions as they will kill a hyena but will not eat it. Hyenas will kill lion cubs and eat them. Finally, there is the African buffalo. This is a huge beast that is extremely aggressive. A group of buffalo will charge any lion, but a buffalo is vulnerable if alone. We must stay away from all of them."

The young men waited until the pride of lions casually walked away. Our leader stood up, keeping a watchful eye in the direction of the lions. Once he felt it was safe, he motioned for everyone to stand. We resumed our walk toward the village as he continued to sweep his long stick in front of him, making sure the path was clear of snakes or any other poisonous creatures.

We reached the area where the baboons were foraging earlier, but there was not a single baboon in sight. Azizi said, "There is something wrong. Either there is a predator in the area or the lions have scared the baboons off. We need to be very careful. Keep your eyes and ears open."

We walked quietly around the big boulders, some as high

as six or seven meters. Everyone was looking around, but I noticed that no one was looking up toward the top of the boulders.

"There!" I said, pointing at a boulder that was about one hundred meters away. All we could see was a long spotted tail. It was that of a leopard, and it was swishing back and forth.

"Oh, yes. I see it," Azizi said with amazement. "Leopards like to scare the baboons, but they know better than to try to take one. Male baboons are capable of using their sharp teeth to attack leopards. Since leopards are also afraid of us, we will proceed quietly."

The column continued on, but when the leader of the column made it around another large bolder, he stopped dead in his tracks. The second man in the column ran into his back. It would have been funny if it were not for the reason the leader stopped.

There, standing right in front of him, was Zar. The great lion's ears went back as he issued a deep, thunderous growl. His beautiful white hair stood up on end, his muscles bulged, and his posture signaled an attack. None of the young men in column was armed with anything more than a blowgun, and they knew that the lion could kill them even after being hit by several of the poisoned darts.

Seeing Zar, Azizi and I ran to the front of the line. I stood firmly with my hands on my hips and my feet spread apart, and said, "Zar! No!" I was scared to death, and without Arlee being present, I hoped he would still remember me.

Zar sniffed the air, and his ears went up immediately. Everyone saw him begin to relax. I walked up to Zar and offered him the back of my hand to smell. Azizi did the same. The rest of the young men were motionless.

Zar sat down and let Azizi and I rub and scratch his massive body. He soon stood up and rubbed his head against my stomach. Then, he walked away in the direction of his pride.

The Voyagers Series

The young men in the column stared at us intently. Azizi acted quickly, knowing that they would think that some sort of magic had been involved. To them, no one would dare trying to play with the king of beasts, especially one with such a bad reputation. He briefly explained to me what he was going to say to his men.

Looking squarely at them, Azizi said, "Listen to me. No magic was involved in what you saw. Arlee and David saved this lion's life before they arrived at the village. The lion was dying after it finally got caught in one of our snares. Once they freed the cat, they used the same leaves to help save his life that they used to save my life. That allowed them to create a special bond with the mighty lion. On the night of the full moon, Arlee and David waited for this lion to come, seeking to take one of our cattle. They asked me to stay away, but I had to see for myself. When the lion came, he recognized them and did not take one of our animals. Arlee showed the cat that I was a friend, and he allowed me to touch him. The only reason we were able to pet the cat is that Arlee and David had saved his life. Do you understand me?"

They all understood, and a sense of relief overcame them. As Azizi and I stood side-by-side, the other men surrounded us and could not stop talking. They had accepted Azizi's explanation, but I knew that they would be quick to tell the villagers when we returned. Azizi would have a lot more explaining to do.

The column started off for the village with everyone still chatting. I saw in the actions of the young men that their respect for Azizi had grown, but Azizi did not let their homage go to his head. He maintained a sense of humility that made me even more proud of him.

As we reached the gate of the village, Chief Ade was waiting for us. The chief commanded Azizi to follow him. Sensing trouble, I began to look for Arlee. When I got to the center of the village, I found her sitting alone next to some bowls.

"Arlee, what are you doing?" I asked.

"Making us some <u>jewelry</u>, but we really need to talk," she said, looking troubled.

"What is wrong?" I asked.

CHAPTER QUESTIONS

1. Why are so many African animals listed as endangered?

2. What makes Azizi a good teacher for Arlee and David?

4. What three conditions do the warriors consider while hunting in the jungle?

5. Why is it important to remain downwind of predatory animals?

6. What is the size of Kenya, in square kilometers?

7. What is the population of Kenya?

8. What is the Cape of Good Hope?

9. In what countries do the *Maasai* live?

10. What parts of Africa are still unexplored?

TRIVIA QUESTION

Who are some famous people from Africa?

CROSSWORD PUZZLES & GAMES

www.thevoyagers.net

Now that you have read the Chapter, answered the Chapter Questions, and researched the Trivia Question, it's time to go to our website! Click the PUZZLES tab and follow the directions. Remember, the underlined words in the chapter are the answers to the online CROSSWORD PUZZLE! You may want to write them down, as one of them is your CODE to play the online GAME!

HAVE FUN!

CHAPTER 7

Jean gasped as she entered the cave. "This is more incredible than I had imagined!" she said with a big smile.

"Dad, look over there," Drew said.

Peter aimed his flashlight as he carefully walked around the waterfall and into the room where the book-filled trunk was sitting. Slowly, he opened the lid and read the letter that was on top of the first book.

"We have only looked at the first two books," Erin said.

Peter picked up **Book 1, Europe** and examined it. After handing it to Drew, he looked at **Book 2, Africa** and took his time turning the pages. He asked Erin to hold it as he started to pick up the third volume. His eyes opened wide, and he placed it carefully back into the truck.

"What you have found is extremely valuable," Peter stated. "Some of these books are hundreds of years old. The third book is so fragile that you could have easily damaged the material that it is made from if you had handled it. May I suggest something to you both?"

"Of course, Dad," Erin and Drew said, practically at the same time.

"What you have found is yours to do with as you wish, but if you find it agreeable, I would be happy to contact my friend, Mr. Taylor, who is the curator of the museum downtown. I would ask to have his team come here and carefully remove the books. They have the technology to digitize and preserve the contents. I would also ask Mr. Taylor to create exact duplicates of everything, including the trunk, and return them to the cave. The original trunk and books would be placed under lock and key in the museum. In this way, the historical items would be protected, and you would remain as the owners of record, having the right to decide what to do with them later. As I said, this is solely your find and your decision," Peter concluded.

"That sounds very reasonable, Dad. Thank you!" Erin said.

"I knew we could count on you to suggest something we would not have thought of," Drew said gratefully.

"I am glad that we agree, and I am thrilled to be involved! While I step outside to make a call, I know that your mother would like to enjoy the waterfall a little longer," Peter suggested as he headed for the entrance.

After pointing out the features of the cave to their mother, Erin said, "Drew, we were getting close to the end of **Book 2, Africa**, and I'm wondering how long this process of making copies will take."

"That's a good point, Erin," Drew said. "I really don't want to be held in suspense for very long!"

"Well, I have an idea," Jean said with a gleam in her eye. "When your father comes back in, I will see what he thinks."

"Okay, Mom. This place is always full of surprises!" Erin said hopefully.

"Here he comes," Drew observed.

"Mr. Taylor is beside himself with anticipation!" Peter reported. "He and his team should be able to begin their work tomorrow afternoon."

"That's wonderful, dear," Jean said, "But the children were getting near the end of **Book 2, Africa**, and I have an idea as to how they may finish it before the books are removed from the cave. I noticed that you seemed quite comfortable in handling the second book. Would it be possible to take digital photos of the remaining pages before we leave the cave? The camera is right here in my pocket!"

Erin and Drew looked at each other and then at their mother.

"Way to go, Mom!" Drew said.

"What do you say, Dad. Is that alright?" Erin pleaded.

"Absolutely!" Peter said with a huge grin. "But you must promise to fill me in on what happened in both books!"

"It's a deal!" Drew said.

After taking the photos, the family was excited to get back and make paper copies. For the first time, Erin and Drew would soon have the privilege of reading the adventure in the comfort of their own home.

~ Book 2, Africa ~

The Cub

As David sat down beside me, I began to explain what had happened while he and the other young men were on the hunting trip with Azizi.

"Zar and his family came to the outskirts of the village. The men were going to try to kill them with spears, but I stopped them before they went outside the front gate. David, it was amazing! I went over to Zar, and when he recognized me, he relaxed. I think he told his family to relax, as well. Even though some of the female lions seemed to be upset, they sat down when Zar sat. He let me hug him and ruffle his mane. In his own way, he introduced me to his family. It was another unbelievable experience for me, but the men and women of the village now think that I am some kind of freak, and I am worried that they no longer trust us," I explained, handing a newly-made bracelet and necklace to David.

David seemed very distracted. He merely accepted the items and slipped them into his leather pouch without really looking at them. All he said was, "Thank you." He appeared to be deep in thought, but in view of what I had just said about Zar and his pride, I was expecting more of a response.

A few moments later, we were completely surrounded by some of the warriors. The men appeared to be exceptionally angry and frightened. We saw the poles going back up. I slowly rose to my feet and bowed to the warriors. I saw David's hand move toward his sword, but he apparently realized that the attempt would be futile.

Within moments, we were once again hanging by our wrists from the tall vertical poles. But this time, the warriors had started to place piles of wood below our feet at the base of the poles.

"They are going to burn us to death! Azizi! Azizi! Where are you?" David screamed.

It was a frenzied scene, with people dancing around us as they sang and chanted. Someone in the crowd threw a stone at me, narrowly missing. At that very moment, Chief Ade emerged from his hut, and everyone stopped what they were doing.

Chief Ade said a few stern words, and then, his son came forth. Chief Ade and Azizi walked toward us, followed by the column of young men that he and David had gone hunting with. With his father at his side, Azizi addressed the village for the first time. Alice had the courage to stand within earshot of us to translate Azizi's words.

"I know that many of you were frightened after seeing Arlee play with the great white lion. As a people with a great knowledge of the land and its animals, we know better than to play with the king of beasts, but perhaps for the first and last time, an unusual thing has happened. The day that Arlee and David arrived in our land, they found the great white lion dying after being caught in one of the snares that we had planted for him. Arlee and David love animals as much as we do, and they risked their lives to save the great cat by removing the snare from his leg. They also used their leaves to help him heal."

The people remained absolutely silent as they listened to Azizi.

"The lion was so grateful that he befriended Arlee and David. This is something that has never happened before, even in our legends. He risked all that he knew about humans and allowed Arlee and David to enter his life. As you know, Arlee and David saved my life, too, and since that time, I have spent every day with these two amazing people. Let me assure you, they are not witches or 'bad blood.' They are our friends, and we have taken them into our homes."

Azizi approached the poles and climbed onto the wood as we dangled beside him. He continued, "After Arlee and David told me about the great white lion, I asked if they knew of a way to keep the great beast away from our cattle. They agreed to try and teach the lion to spare our animals. On the night of the full moon, they went outside our village, next to our cattle, and waited for the lion. They told me to stay away, but I had to see for myself. I went to our front gate to watch. Right on time, the great white lion appeared, but when he saw his two friends, he did not attack any of our cattle. Instead, he sat down and played with Arlee and David. It took everything I had, but I walked out to them. At first, the lion jumped up to protect them from me, but when he saw Arlee hug me, the great cat also allowed me to approach and touch him. I had never been so scared."

A few gasps could be heard among the villagers at Azizi's

revelation.

"On the way back from hunting today, we ran straight into the great white lion once again. He was on his way to catch up to his family. He would have attacked us if he had not recognized David and me by our scent," Azizi continued.

The young men who had witnessed this all confirmed Azizi's story and assured the villagers that Azizi spoke the truth.

Our wrists were burning with pain as Azizi <u>wrapped</u> his arms around us and said to his people, "One day, with your consent, I will take my father's place and be the chief of our tribe. I will do everything to make sure that I provide you with the same great leadership that my father has. Also, as two of you know, I have found a cave on the side of the mountain. This cave was filled with gold, but after the volcano blast, the cave is concealed by lava. What none of you know is that each time I visited the cave over the years, I removed a large chunk of gold and hid it."

David and I looked at each other, surprised that Azizi would bring this up.

"That gold belongs to this village, and whenever we need it, I will uncover a piece. I stand here between my two best friends, and I ask that you allow them to remain in our lives. They are just like us. They want to be loved as they love you. If you do not accept them, then burn us all now!" Azizi declared.

There was complete silence and no one moved. The chief was so proud of how his son had addressed the village that he climbed up onto the pile of wood and put his arms around all three of them. Then, with great <u>boldness</u>, he announced, "I believe my son, and I am willing to risk my life as well."

At this point, the young men who had gone hunting with Azizi moved over and sat in a circle around the pole where David, Azizi, the chief, and I were standing. It was one of the bravest and most unselfish acts that David and I have ever witnessed. We both shed tears of gratitude.

Soon the elders of the village worked together to get David and me down from the poles. Everyone wanted to hug us. The chief ordered another party, and the village sprang to life. As smiles returned to their faces, many of the villagers stood and talked with Azizi. The chief beckoned Alice to come closer, and they both approached us. Alice repeated the chief's statement, saying, "You have saved my son, and you have also brought our village back together again. Consider this your home."

When he finished, I looked at Alice for assistance as I addressed the chief. "Chief Ade, even though we had the opportunity to make a unique bond with the great white lion, we must emphasize that this connection between the cat and the three of us is a delicate relationship. My brother and I understand that lions are wild and dangerous animals, and anyone attempting to imitate our actions to form a similar bond will surely die. We believe that the great white lion has made your village part of his territory. Please remove all the snares and let him guard you for as long as he is alive, but tell your people to continue to respect the lions. Make sure no one goes near the pride."

Alice said, "These are the chief's words, 'I understand. The relationship is between you and David, not my son. You saved the lion's life, and for doing that, you have a friendship with the king of beasts. Tonight, I will tell our people a story that was handed down by my ancestors. It will explain how fortunate we are to have the great white lion in our territory and why we have not killed him long before now.'"

As Azizi approached us, Alice also translated what the chief said to Azizi. "Son, if you believe what I will declare to everyone tonight, then not only will you be a great leader, but your village will prosper."

After we all hugged one another, David and I began walking toward our huts to rest before eating. David turned to me and said, "This has been quite a day! I guess you know now why I was stunned when you said that Zar had approached the village. I was thinking about the encounter that our group also had with him earlier! I know we had agreed with Azizi to keep our relationship with Zar a secret, but that has been overruled by Zar himself!"

"Just like the two ill-intentioned men and the volcano overruled our pact to keep the gold a secret!" I said. We both laughed, and David suggested that we sit down for a few minutes. He reached into his leather pouch and pulled out the jewelry that I had made.

"I did not get to hear how your day went before all of the drama happened!" David said apologetically. "I know that these were the beautiful results, though," he continued, gazing at the colorful adornments.

"Oh, thank you for remembering, David. It is good to have a few moments to relax and talk. My day started out innocently enough. I spent time with a group of five young women who were doing all kinds of things in the village. I could tell that they were close friends, and they talked the entire time they were doing the chores. I learned that doing these chores is the role of every woman in the village. They sewed, cleaned the huts, cooked, and took care of the babies. Besides that, they fetched water, cleaned the clothes, and made beautiful jewelry out of the various items that the older men had carved and polished."

"As a matter of fact, I also learned about what the older men do to prepare the parts of the animals that the women use in jewelry-making," David added.

"Teamwork!" I said.

"Yes, but it seems like the women are doing a lot of the work inside the village!" David observed.

"Absolutely! I know that the men do the hunting, but they also spend a considerable time talking in the village!" I added.

"With all of the dangers out on the savanna and in the jungle, there is always something to talk about!" David said.

"Right, and by the way, I found out why you encountered manure on the roof of the chief's hut when you were drilling a hole to get the crushed leaves and honey down to Azizi. I saw one of the women go to the cattle pen and fill a basket with dung. Then, she climbed onto the roof of one of the huts and began spreading it around with her hands like mud. I asked Akilah, the woman who was beside me at the time, why this was done. Akilah explained to me that manure is strong when it dries, and it helps repel insects and bugs, but it cannot be smelled inside."

"That's a blessing!" David exclaimed.

"Then, Akilah asked me if I would like to help make some jewelry, and I jumped at the chance. Her name means "intelligent one who knows," and she was a good teacher! She gave me several pieces string of varying length. The string was made of strong grass that had been tightly woven together. Akilah had me sit with three other young women who were doing the same thing. Ten bowls, each filled with different items, were in front of me. Some bowls contained different brightly-colored glass beads, while others held polished bones. There were crocodile teeth, coarse giraffe hairs,   various small seashells, and ostrich egg shells that had been sanded into round pieces. Akilah instructed me to tie a knot at one end of the string and start adding things from the different bowls. Every piece already had a hole in the middle of it."

"They use quite a variety of items," David remarked.

"Yes," I said, "And Akilah said that sometimes they make jewelry to remind them of something special. She asked me to take my time and make a necklace and a bracelet for myself and one of each for you. At first, I was uncomfortable about using bones or teeth, but I began to understand that in this country, the people live side-by-side with the animals. I wanted to make some things that would remind us of the many wonderful people that we have met, as well the many different animals that we have encountered here in Africa."

"Thanks, Arlee. I will cherish what you made for me," Brain said, giving me a hug.

"And just after Akilah showed me how to close the necklaces and bracelets, Zar and his pride showed up!" I exclaimed. "I ran to the edge of the village to see what was happening, and you have heard the rest! When the men and women of the village witnessed my interaction with Zar and his pride, they were confused and scared. As we walked back to the village, everyone kept their distance, and no one would speak to me. I returned to finish the jewelry, and only one woman came over to me. Her name is Afra, which means 'peaceful.' She comforted me by explaining why the people were afraid, and I told her about how we had initially met Zar. I told her that I understood how easily misunderstandings arise between people, and I suggested that you and Azizi would be able to explain more when you returned from hunting."

"And that is when everything broke loose!" David said with a big laugh. "It is time to get a little rest. All finally ended well!"

After we napped, David and I headed toward the center of

the town to see what we could do to help. We also needed to find someone to show us how to wear the jewelry properly.

The necklaces were both were alike. In the middle of each was one large lion's claw, followed on each side with one red and three black beads, followed by three crocodile teeth, followed by four black beads and one white bead. Next, there were five beautifully-polished, multi-colored bones, with a black bead between each of them. Finally, there were two <u>seashells</u>, followed by a few variously-colored beads.

While walking among the villagers, I shared with David what each piece meant to me. "In our necklaces, the claws, teeth, and bones represent the animals of Africa. The black beads symbolize the people, the red beads represent the struggle to survive, the seashells symbolize peace and tranquility, and the multi-colored beads show the overall beauty of Africa. Our bracelets are made of polished white bones. The bones represent the respect that these people have for all of the animals in Africa."

"You really captured the essence of this place and its people, Arlee," David said.

As we came to the center of town, everyone smiled at us. Once again, we were part of the village. One of the girls who had made a necklace with me saw that we needed some help. She approached us and <u>demonstrated</u> how to tie the necklaces on. Azizi came over to admire our jewelry and gave us both a hug.

"One of our treasured customs is storytelling. It is my father's responsibility to pass on the stories of our ancestors. It helps us remember where we came from and who we are as a tribe. Tonight, he will tell us all a story," Azizi explained.

"We will be happy to learn about the history of your tribe! May we with help with anything in the village?" I asked.

"No, thank you, my sister. Please sit down next to my father's hut and watch the sun disappear. I will get you something to drink while you wait for the feast," Azizi said graciously.

David and I were willing to help, but Azizi wanted us to observe how the village functioned. His facial expression reflected how proud he was of his people – grandparents, fathers, mothers, brothers, and sisters who were all working toward a common goal. It was clear to us, that under his father's continuing guidance, Azizi would become a great leader.

As the light of the sun disappeared, a large fire was lit. Chief Ade and his wife came out and sat in their chairs next to us. Azizi took a place on the other side of us and said it would be his privilege to interpret each word of his father's story after the feast.

When the food was ready, the people of the village patiently waited as Chief Ade and his wife were served first, then Azizi, followed by David and me. After everyone had finished their food and water, the entire village gathered in a circle around the fire with Chief Ade.

The chief rose and slammed one end of his beautiful staff into the ground. Everyone stopped talking and looked respectfully at him. It was time for him to begin to his story.

"I am going to repeat something that my great grandfather told his people and my father told me. While this story is very old, you will see how it relates to us today. As you listen to my words and see my true heart, this story will come alive."

The chief paused and looked and David and me.

"Before I start, I want our new friends to understand that our country is under siege. Many of our brothers and sisters are being forced to leave our land and become slaves in other parts of the world. People come here and kill our animals for sport. We have no way to defend ourselves but to hide. Yet, regarding those that do cross our path peaceably, we have tried to educate them about our land. I have also heard that men are being assembled to come and cut down our trees in order to sell the wood elsewhere. I cannot explain what possesses some men to do this to other men. I fear for our future and our way of life, and when I go, I have to leave this terrible reality to my son. I hope that you can find a way to protect our tribe and all of the people of Africa. It is a burden that no father wishes to pass on to his son. Please forgive me," the chief said, dropping his head.

It was a solemn moment that touched everyone. Azizi continued to interpret for us as his father looked out at the villagers.

"Now, let me tell you a story that I have never told you before. Many years ago, my great grandfather told his people about a great white lion. He said that the white lion was sacred and would bring prosperity and good fortune to any village that he chose as his territory. He said our ancestors believed that when a white star fell to the ground, a white lion was born. For years, my great grandfather wished for this to happen. There was little food for his people, and water was hard to find. They were struggling to survive, but every night, he would ask for a white star to fall.

"One night, he walked outside, looked up into the night sky, and shook his fist at the stars. He was desperate because the people in his village were starving. At that same moment, a white star fell to the ground. He believed that a white male baby lion had been born. He told his people that he and his eldest son were going to search for the cub. He told them that when he found the animal, he would have his son watch over the young lion to keep him safe. He also told the villagers that things would get much better for everyone.

"The next day, my great grandfather and my grandfather left the village to find the special cub. They knew all of the prides in the area and planned to check on each pride, one by one, to see if they could find the baby white lion.

"They found the first pride after a half day walk, and all the lionesses were there. There was no baby white lion. They continued on to the next pride, and found the same situation. With only two prides left in their territory, my great grandfather was beginning to lose hope.

"At the end of the second day, they found the third pride and noticed that one of the lionesses was gone. There could be a number of reasons why she was not with her pride, but great grandfather believed that she was <u>nursing</u> her new cubs. He knew that if he did not find the cubs soon, it might be too late to save the baby white lion. To great grandfather, this was a life-or-death situation, not only for the white lion cub, but for his people."

As Chief Ade was telling his story, he was in magnificent form. He had a beautifully spotted leopard's hide wrapped around his waist that fell all the way to his ankles. The lion's hide that was draped over his right shoulder was belted at his waist, and he was wearing hundreds of multi-colored beads around his neck. His headband was gold, and it had colorful chips of gems throughout it. He was a large man, and when he stood in front of the village, he looked so strong for his age. But as powerful and knowledgeable as he was, he remained humble in dealing with his people.

As he walked around the fire, Chief Ade used his staff, his arms, and his hands to emphasize his story. He was careful to make eye contact with everyone as he spoke. The only sounds that could be heard were the crackling of the fire and Chief Ade's deep and soothing voice. The people were attentive to every word.

"My great grandfather and grandfather looked for many hiding places where lionesses were known to raise their cubs, but they found nothing. As the sun's light was fading, they came to the last hiding place that they were able to reach that day. My great grandfather saw some movement, and both of the men knelt down and waited to see what it was. They stayed a good distance from the hiding place, and they were careful to be downwind. Soon their efforts were rewarded as a lioness stood up and yawned. Under her legs were three little cubs. To the amazement and relief of my great grandfather and grandfather, there in plain sight, barely able to walk, was a white lion cub.

"Having given my grandfather careful <u>instructions</u>, my great grandfather walked off toward the village, leaving my grandfather alone to watch over the cubs. Most cubs that die early are those that are caught playing outside of their den in their mother's absence. Even though the mother will protect her cubs with her life, she must feed herself, and it is when she feeds that the cubs are at the greatest risk.

"Thankfully, nothing happened to the cubs that night. The next morning, the mother came back to the cubs to feed them. Day followed day, and to my grandfather's delight, no threats came to the cubs. As he watched them grow, they ventured farther and farther from the den while their mother was not in sight. This frightened my grandfather.

"When my great grandfather arrived back at the village, he told everyone that he had found a baby white lion. He also told his tribe that they must move closer to where the white lion cub was living. Although the tribe did not want to move, they gathered their things and followed my great grandfather for many days over the savanna to find a new location closer to the white lion cub.

"To the good fortune of my great grandfather's tribe, they came upon a small <u>stream</u> of fresh water that bubbled up through the ground. The stream was no wider than a man, but the water was sufficient to support many of the wild animals of the savanna as well as the tribe. The people began building new huts. They all drank from and bathed in the stream, and for the first time in many years, the villagers began to be hopeful.

"The people of the tribe started to believe that the story about the white lion was true after all. Each day, a few of the warriors followed the stream away from their new village and were thankful for the ample water supply and the fact that the stream attracted many wild animals that they could hunt as food.

"The little white lion continued to grow, and he would soon be introduced to his pride. When that day came, the rest of the pride did not know what to think of the feisty little white lion. The other cubs were curious, and they would play roughly with the white cub. The white male was undeterred and did not let the other cubs gain superiority over him. He was bold and growing stronger by the day. He would go to his father, the male lion that ruled the pride, and play with him constantly. At first, the huge male lion did not know what to make of his strange-looking cub. But in time, the male lion became good friends with his unique son who continued to grow at an amazing rate. He stood out from all of his brothers and sisters, not only in color, but in size and strength, as well.

"As we all know, lions are nomads, and their territories are sometimes vast. In my great grandfather's day, just as in ours, the lions moved from one part of their territory to another. From time to time, an unknown male lion would wander into the pride's territory, and the male leader of the pride would have to defend his group. Fortunately for the white lion, his father was big and strong, and he successfully defended his pride several times.

"Almost a year later, two lions that were brothers came to challenge the white lion's father. These two lions were known as 'the evil twins.' The white lion's father was no match for the evil twins, and they ran him off, along with all of the other adult male lions in the pride. They killed all of the cubs except the white cub who was able to escape the rampage.

"The next few weeks would determine the white lion's fate.

He had never made his own kill before, and if he did not make one soon, he would starve to death. The white lion was alone and getting desperate. It had been two weeks since he had eaten. He was losing strength, and he knew he had to make a kill. While lying in the tall grass, he heard something close by. Quietly, he lifted his head to see what was causing the noise. It was a family of wild guinea fowl. At this point, he was so hungry he did not care what it was. He had to eat. This was his chance, and with all his strength, he got up and went after the animals. He was able to catch one, and although the meal was small, it was his first kill. It gave him both sustenance and confidence.

"The white lion was now on his way to becoming a great leader. He had learned to kill, and as the days turned into weeks, the weeks into months, and the months into years, there was one thing that the white lion always kept in the back of his mind. He wanted revenge for what the evil twins had done to his father and his pride.

"The white lion had grown larger than any lion on the savanna, and his prowess was unmatched. The day finally came when the white lion challenged the evil twins. It was a fight that could be heard at a great distance and it lasted for quite some time. Ultimately, the more powerful and younger white lion defeated the evil twins, driving them out of his territory. But a lion's life is always short. Even though this white lion lived longer than most, the day eventually came when he also died.

"Soon thereafter, my great grandfather became ill, and the small stream dried up. My grandfather became the leader after his father's death. Under the circumstances, he believed that the tribe needed to move closer to the big mountain in order to have a better chance of finding another stream of clean water. The village was on the move again. As all of you know, my grandfather found this spot for us to live and prosper. Were there other white lions that existed in between? We will never know, but we do know that a great white lion has lived with us for years, and we have prospered."

With that, the chief sat down and everyone started shouting for joy. Laughter, tears, and genuine happiness rippled through the village. As people mingled about, we told Azizi how much we appreciated the warmth and love of his people, and during the rest of the evening, we enjoying ourselves immensely. But in our hearts, we knew that we had to leave soon.

Bright and early the next morning, Azizi awakened us from a deep sleep. "Come on! It is time to go to the mountain again. You still have a lot to learn," he said exuberantly.

There was no argument, and we were soon ready to start walking. As we crossed the stream and headed for the mountain, we were met by the two men who had followed us to the cave. They looked <u>angry</u> and started making threatening gestures with their hands and spears. They spoke loudly to Azizi in their native tongue, and my brother and I stepped back and readied ourselves to defend Azizi with David's sword and my bow and arrows. But Azizi said something calmly to the men and they seemed to have accepted whatever he had said. Azizi turned to us, saying, "This will be otherwise resolved. Please follow me."

We could only conclude that the two men were forcing Azizi to reveal where he had hidden the gold.

"We are all going back to the village, where I must retrieve a map," Azizi said, winking at us with his back turned to the men.

When we got back to the village, Azizi went inside his hut. The two men stood behind us, talking nervously and waiting impatiently for their evil plan to come to fruition. Soon, Azizi returned with a piece of paper. As he handed the paper to the two men, Chief Ade appeared. The chief yelled something, and the two men were instantly surrounded by several other warriors.

The warriors tied the hands of the two men together. Before long, the entire village had gathered to see what was happening. Chief Ade explained to the villagers that the two men were trying to force Azizi to tell them where he had hidden the gold so that they could steal it. The chief declared that the two men were no longer a part of the tribe, and that they were being forcibly cast out. If they were ever seen near the village again, they would be hunted down and killed.

The horror on the faces of the two men was apparent. They were escorted by the other warriors to the front gate of the village. The warriors opened the gate, pushed the two men outside, and then closed the gated. The two men knew they would have to elude the *Baka* and cross the river filled with danger. They also knew that even if they were able to do these two things, they would have to deal with whatever nature brought their way, and they had no spears or shields in their possession.

Azizi was not at all surprised. He told us that there was no map showing where the gold was hidden. The only map was the one in his head. Since he had declared the existence of the hidden gold to his whole tribe the day before, he was expecting something like this to happen. He had formulated a plan and discussed it with his father overnight, after they had retired to their hut.

Once again, we headed for the mountain and arrived at our favorite place with the view of the entire savanna. Azizi brought along some food and water, and as we were eating, he explained more aspects of the savanna and the jungle. He said that the biggest problem we faced was getting across the river. There was no longer a tree bridge. On the one hand, this was good, because it helped protect the village from other tribes that might wander across and happen upon us, but on the other hand, it was bad for our tribe. That bridge had been our only safe way to cross the river.

"Can we simply cut down another tree that will span the banks of the river?" David asked.

"Yes, I believe you will be able to use your sword to do just that. However, before you even make it to the river, you will have to go through the darkest part of the jungle where the *Baka* live. I will provide you with shields, and as you recall from your first journey through this area with our warriors, you must run side-by-side as fast as you can so the darts will not hit you. It will be a run for your lives," Azizi reminded us with his head down.

"Once you get across the river, you will have to walk through another jungle. The jungle on the other side of the river does not have *Baka*, but it is still full of danger. You must find a long stick to sweep back and forth in front of you as you walk. One of you needs to be looking up into the trees while the other is looking down on the ground. Danger is everywhere in the jungle, and it never lets up. I do not know much about the jungle across the river, except for stories that my father has told. Please remember what I have taught you."

"You make it sound as though it is impossible to get back to the port," said David.

"What I am saying is that you must work together," Azizi replied.

For awhile, the three of us sat quietly, looking out over the jungle and the savanna and keeping our thoughts to ourselves.

Then Azizi stood up and faced us. His voice was full of emotion as he said, "I want to explain something important to both of you. I can tell you as much as I know about the jungle, the river, and the savanna, but no matter how much I relate to you about the various things that you might encounter, it is not a substitute for experience. It takes years of living here in Africa to learn what to do and what not to do. Learning the different plant species and remembering what you can eat and what is poisonous could take a lifetime. You must rely on your wits and get off the savanna as quickly as possible. I will do everything I can to help you get started, but ultimately you will be on your own. I have seen your ingenuity, my brother and sister, and in my heart, I know that you are capable of making it. If by some chance you come here again, please know that this is your home and that everyone in the village thinks of you as members of our tribe and their family."

I could not hold my tears any longer. "Every moment of every day was a learning experience with your tribe, Azizi," I said. "But above all, we have learned to love you dearly!"

"We are certainly going to miss you, Azizi," David said with his eyes glistening.

The three of us continued to look out over the jungle and savanna without talking. It was enough to know that the three of us were together, taking in some of the most beautiful scenery in the world. With Azizi keenly noting the position of the sun, we stood up and started back to the village.

CHAPTER QUESTIONS

1. Besides wearing jewelry, how else do people personalize their appearance?

2. Do you have any items of jewelry that represent something

special?

3. Is it better to follow or lead?

4. Does your family observe particular customs or traditions?

5. What is the mean temperature in Kenya?

6. What responsibilities do the women of the *Kikuyu* tribe assume?

7. How many time zones is Kenya from your home?

8. What is the largest lake in Kenya?

9. How many different languages are spoken in Africa?

10. Why is storytelling important to Chief Ade and his tribe?

TRIVIA QUESTION

What is Africa's largest country, geographically?

CROSSWORD PUZZLES & GAMES
www.thevoyagers.net
Now that you have read the Chapter, answered the Chapter Questions, and researched the Trivia Question, it's time to go to our website! Click the PUZZLES tab and follow the directions. Remember, the underlined words in the chapter are the answers to the online CROSSWORD PUZZLE! You may want to write them down, as one of them is your CODE to play the online GAME!

HAVE FUN!

CHAPTER 8

"I would really enjoy making some jewelry in the way Arlee did," Erin said.

"Right, but don't expect me to hunt for the animals!" Drew said as he flopped into his favorite chair in the family room.

"If we ever go to Africa, I hope we meet someone like Azizi," Erin said as she rounded the corner into the kitchen.

"I would enjoy meeting someone with his character anywhere!" Drew added, raising his voice a little so Erin could still hear him. "It's so much fun learning about the customs of other people. I like the way Arlee and David respected the villagers and their way of life. It would be nice if more people would do that."

"No doubt about it!" Erin said, returning with her hands full. "Here's some popcorn and a cold drink for you. It's just a little treat after finishing the morning chores!"

"Thanks! It's time to find out what happens next in the village," Drew said. "Will you please do the reading from our printed copy of the book? My fingers are covered with butter already!"

~ Book 2, Africa ~

The Snake

As we walked down the mountain, nobody said much. The prospect of parting was weighing heavily on each of us. When we were able to see the village, we noticed that people were running around, and as we got closer, we could hear screams and crying. Azizi bolted, and Arlee and I tried to keep up with him.

When we approached the circle of the huts, Azizi came to a stop. The people of the village ran toward him in great distress. They dropped to their knees and kissed his feet, crying hysterically. Azizi stepped aside and ran toward his hut. Although many of the villagers were surrounding it, they left the doorway clear for him. Arlee and I stood at the opening to the hut. Azizi entered quietly and found his mother kneeling next to his father, who was lying down. She was sobbing and holding his hand. His father did not move, nor did he breathe. He seemed to be in a peaceful sleep.

Azizi knelt next to his mother and stared at his father's face. Arlee began to cry and looked at me for answers. Alice got up from her chair and came over to hug both of us.

"Azizi, what can we do?" I asked softly.

"Please, my dear friends, leave us alone for awhile," he replied.

I took Arlee's hand as we left Chief Ade's hut. I suggested that we walk to the stream to be alone.

"David, can we help in any way?" pleaded Arlee.

"There is nothing we can do," I conceded. "Even if we had a great quantity of melaleuca leaves, we could not help. They are meant for bites, cuts, and sicknesses, but not death."

Begrudgingly, Arlee agreed. "Yes, David. We can only offer

our steadfast support to Azizi as he abides by the customs of his tribe. He will be a wonderful leader."

We spent a short time by the peaceful stream, trying to prepare ourselves for the emotional challenges ahead.

"We should go back now," Arlee said.

As we entered the village, several people came to us and got on their knees to ask us for help. Both Arlee and I hugged each of them with tears in our eyes. Even without a word, the people seemed to understand that in the face of death, there was nothing we could do.

Amidst all of the villagers, we sat outside the chief's hut, waiting for someone to appear. It was a long time before Alice emerged. She looked at everyone, and with a peaceful expression on her face, she spoke in their native tongue. "Chief Ade has joined the ranks of his ancestors." Many of the people began to sob. Alice walked over to where we were standing, knowing that we would need a translator.

Azizi came through the doorway of the hut with his mother following behind him. Azizi seemed to be composed. In their native tongue, he addressed his tribe.

"It is hard for me to say this, because my best friend, mentor, and father has passed. He died in his sleep, and Alice believes it may have been due to a <u>mosquito</u> bite, but she is not sure. It appears that he did not suffer.

"My father had talked to me about his eventual death on several occasions, but I always thought that its occurrence would be far in the future. His words to me were always the same. He said that if I was to be a good leader, I must listen to the majority of my tribe. I must not make decisions quickly, and if possible, I should wait a day before finalizing an important decision. Lastly, he said that I must consider all of the perceived consequences, both good and bad, that might result from the decisions I make."

"More than once, my father said, 'I do not know why I feel

that my time is near, but do not be fearful or sad. When your day comes, I urge you to ask the people of the village what they want.' Therefore, I stand here in front of you today and ask, 'Do you want me to take my father's place?'"

All of the villagers rose to their feet, and every single person said, "Yes." There was no doubt in anyone's mind that Azizi would be the best chief for the tribe. In an unprecedented expression of <u>obedience</u>, everyone got down on their knees and bowed to their new leader.

Azizi was humbled by the actions of his tribe. He asked them to rise, and once again, he addressed them.

"With all my heart, I pledge my intention to lead the way my father did. I cannot do it alone. I will need your help. Together, we will strive to make decisions that will enable our village to <u>prosper</u> and be safe from the evils that surround us.

"Now, according to our tribal customs, we will perform the ceremonial burial for my father. As we prepare for this occasion, I ask that you not be sad. My father had always had expressed a desire to go to his ancestors knowing that you, his brothers and sisters, remained happy. That was most important to him.

"I ask that you to listen to the things my father taught me about what our ancestors believed about death. Please be seated."

Azizi continued to stand while his mother sat behind him. Everyone else sat down to listen to what Azizi was about to say. Knowing that it was his responsibility to convey his father's wishes, he resumed speaking with gentleness and humility.

"Our ancestors understood death as the beginning of a person's deeper relationship with all of creation. They viewed it as the completion of life, and the beginning of the interaction between the visible and the invisible worlds. They believed that the goal of life is to become an ancestor after death. This is why every member of our tribe who dies is given a specifically prescribed funeral, consisting of a number of ceremonial rites. If this is not done, our forefathers believed that the dead person might become a wandering ghost, unable to live properly after death, and therefore, posing a danger to the living. Proper death rites were seen as more of a promise of protection for the living than a guarantee of safe passage for the dead.

"Most of you have heard that some tribes adhere to the custom of removing a dead body through a hole in the wall of a home, rather than through the door. According to their belief, this is done so the dead person cannot remember the way back to the living, since the hole in the wall is promptly closed. Sometimes, the body is removed feet first, pointing away from the hut. A zigzag path is taken to the burial site, thorns are thrown along the way, and a barrier is built around the grave itself. They do this so the dead person can never find his or her way back.

"Our tribe, however, has traditionally believed that special efforts are to be made to ensure that the person who died is able to return to their home. Some of our ancestors have been buried under or next to their homes. My mother believes in having my father buried near us."

It was amazing to observe Azizi talking to his village. It was as though he had been doing it all of his life. We listened carefully to Alice as she continued to translate.

"Some tribes have different thoughts about what happens after this life. Some believe the dead go to a land which is like this world. Our Kenyan ancestors believed in a single supreme being who is the creator of the earth. They taught that there is a continuation of life after death, but to live here and now has always been the most important thing to our forefathers.

"My father told me that his grandfather taught him that if a person is a wizard, a murderer, a thief, one who has broken the community code or taboos, or one who has had an unnatural death or an improper burial, then that person is be doomed to punishment in the afterlife as a wandering ghost, and will be beaten and expelled by the ancestors or subjected to a period of torture, according to the seriousness of their misdeeds. My father believed that he must follow his ancestors' ways to make sure he is accepted by them.

"My father also believed that death is one of the last transitional stages of life, requiring passage rites that take time to complete. As part of the ritual, we will kill an animal to provide food for our tribe and guests. We will also bury some of my father's personal belongings with him, according to his wishes. Custom dictates that this will help in his journey.

"My father did not wish to bring trouble to us. His desire was for the strengthening of life on the earth. We will have the funeral in the morning before sunrise, since it has long been believed that sorcerers move around in the afternoon, looking for bodies to be used for their evil purposes. As your new chief, please help my mother and I prepare for a funeral in accordance with my father's beliefs."

Not a sound could be heard, and all eyes were riveted on Azizi. It seemed strange that earlier in the day, Azizi was a young man whose greatest concern was helping us get back to the port. Now, he had taken the position of the leader of his tribe in an exhibition of amazing dignity. Being able to witness this transition was such an honor for both Arlee and me.

After Azizi announced that it was time for the funeral preparations to begin, all of the villagers quietly dispersed and began to fulfill their designated duties.

Arlee and I noticed that Alice had started walking toward the stream, and we wanted to thank her for translating for us.

"Alice," I said. "Are you all right?"

"Yes, my dear friends, I am fine. I was thinking of the many times Chief Ade demonstrated kindness to me and how fortunate I was to have found this village. I will miss him."

"Yes, Alice, we can appreciate your fondness for him," I

said. "Thank you for translating Azizi's words. He handled his responsibilities remarkably well. After he finished speaking, Arlee and I looked at each other, and I think it occurred to both of us at the same time that there is something that we would like to discuss with you."

Speaking softly, Arlee said, "On the day that you invited us into your hut, we noticed an open Bible on your table."

"Yes, Arlee, I read it every day," Alice said.

"We each have Bibles back home, too, and may I say that they are well-worn from use," I added.

Arlee continued, "Have you ever shared with Azizi what the Bible says about death?"

"Precious ones, you are very perceptive," Alice said. "When I began to teach the English language to Azizi, I used the Bible. In time, I will teach him more."

"That will be a source of comfort to us on our journey home," I said. We all hugged and headed back toward the village.

"Since you will be leaving tomorrow," Alice said, "I want you both to know that the things you have done for this tribe have been incredible, and words cannot adequately express my appreciation. I am sure that Azizi will continue to do everything in his power to help you."

The three of us sat outside Azizi's hut and waited for him.

Moments later, Azizi appeared. He sat down next to us, and Alice arose to go inside with Azizi's mother.

"Azizi, we are so sorry. Is there anything that we can do?" asked Arlee.

"Thank you for asking, but rather, there are some things that I want to do for you," Azizi said. "I have two shields for you, as promised, and I also want to give you a blowgun with several poisonous darts. You must also have another bag of water. If you ever get in trouble, light a fire and sprinkle water on it to create smoke. I have talked to my mother and some of the elders of our tribe, and if we see any sign of smoke, I will send some of my warriors to come and help you. For now, please sit and watch us prepare for my father's burial. As I mentioned, the burial will be in the morning, and it will not take long. We all hope that you will attend it before you leave."

"We certainly will, Azizi," I assured.

Azizi got up and said a few words to one of the young men of his village. In a few moments, the young man returned with goblets of water and fruit for us. Azizi got up and walked over to a group of villagers that were diligently preparing for the funeral.

"I know Azizi asked us to sit here and watch, but I wish we could be of help," Arlee said with frustration.

"Me too, but we must do as Azizi has asked us out of respect for the customs of the tribe. Tonight, we must be sure to check all of our things. I have a small quantity of leaves left in my container, but I know yours is empty," David said.

"There are so many perils out there. I hope our supply will last!" Arlee said.

"Arlee, we do not know what we may have to face, but we must not doubt that we have been well prepared by Azizi. He has spent a great deal of time imparting his knowledge to us. We simply must make it back to the port," David said.

Soon Azizi came back to sit with us again. "How are my two friends doing?" he asked.

"We are fine, but we wish there was something that we could do to help," Arlee replied.

"I know of something you can do. When you get back home, try to educate your people about what is happening here in Africa. We have talked about the killing of our animals by foreigners. We have talked about the slave ships that take our people away by force. But there are people that come to our land to cut down entire jungles of trees. Our land and its people and animals survive based on a delicate balance. The animals rely on the savanna as well as the jungles, and our people depend on the animals. Because our tribe takes only what we need, we do not upset the balance of nature. But I am afraid that unless we educate our own people and others who visit our land as to what is being inflicted upon our continent, the balance of nature that we and our <u>ancestors</u> have enjoyed will be lost.

Arlee and I looked at each other, and I said, "Azizi, you have our promise that we will tell everyone we know and everyone we meet. We will even find a way to communicate with those that we will never meet! It will become our crusade, fueled by our love and respect for you and your land."

Suddenly, a scream was heard from inside Azizi's hut. We jumped up and ran inside to find Azizi's mother up against the wall, pointing down at some of the hides. Azizi saw a long grey snake with a cream-colored underbody slithering beneath them. I took my sword from its scabbard and slowly walked over to the snake.

"Be careful, David," Azizi warned. "That is a black mamba, one of the most poisonous snakes in our country. That is what must have killed my father, not a mosquito! David, this snake moves incredibly fast and is extremely aggressive when cornered. Arlee, take Mother and Alice outside now!"

Azizi stayed with me, and my sword was ready to kill the snake that killed my best friend's father. Without notice, the snake moved at an incredible speed toward me, but I was ready. My years of practice paid off. I moved to one side as the snake tried to bite me, and my sword found the back of the snake's neck. It was over in a flash. The snake was dead.

Azizi grabbed the body of the snake and walked outside to show the villagers who had gathered outside. I followed, with the head of the snake resting on the end of my sword.

"This is what killed my father. Where there is one black mamba, there is bound to be more," Azizi stated. "I want all of you to check inside your huts for any sign of other snakes. If you find one, do not try to kill it. Get out of your hut as quickly as possible. The warriors and I will take care of it," Azizi commanded.

Everyone left to check their huts, and Azizi commanded that all of the warriors get long sticks and spears. After dispatching them to check the perimeter of the village, Azizi walked up to me, and said, "Thank you. Once again, you have saved the lives of others, and we now know how my father died. A few years ago, he survived the bite of a mosquito, which we call 'the silent death,' but to be bitten by the black mamba is certain death. Please throw the head of the snake into the fire pit. I will give the rest of it to one of our cooks, who will skin it so that we can eat the meat. You may have noticed that the snake was as long as we are tall. Our tribal ritual requires that the skin of the snake be placed at my father's feet when he is buried. Our ancestors taught that this symbolic gesture allows the evil of the black mamba to be stamped out."

I did as Azizi instructed, and as I was about to join Arlee outside of Azizi's hut, we heard a commotion and saw many of the people running to the back of the village. Arlee and I followed them to see what was happening. One of the warriors had found a nest of baby snakes, and at Azizi's bidding, the warriors began to kill them, one by one. With that being accomplished, everyone knew that there was one adult snake left to find.

Azizi told his people to continue looking for the last adult snake. He sat down next to us and began to describe some of the deadly animals of Africa, saying, "The black mamba that killed my father grows to four meters in length and can move almost as fast as a person can run. These snakes are very <u>aggressive</u>, and many times, they will kill animals and not eat them. The king cobra, which lives mainly in South Africa, is even larger and just as aggressive. When it rises up to strike, it flattens out its neck, revealing a beautiful design. In doing so, it tries to appear larger and more intimidating to other animals that want to make a meal of it. Hippos, snakes, crocodiles, lions, and elephants are all killers of our people, but statistically, the most deadly is an insect – the mosquito. When it bites, it transfers blood from one animal or person to the victim. Often times, the blood that it transfers is diseased. As I mentioned, we call the mosquito 'the silent death,' because it is often undetected as it lands on its victims. The mosquito commonly strikes at night when people are asleep. Most victims never knew what bit them."

"It seems hard to believe that there are so many killers in this beautiful land," Arlee said. "Where we come from, there are also deadly animals, but there seems to be many more here."

"Do not forget the rats back home, Arlee. They can grow as large as an elephant," I said with a little laugh. I did not mean to be disrespectful to Azizi by chuckling, but my laughter turned out to be <u>contagious</u>, as Azizi and Arlee joined in. It was a welcome moment of relief after a day of tragedy, sadness, and fear.

Another loud scream from the opposite end of the village jolted us to our feet. By the time Azizi, Arlee, and I got there, one of the warriors had beaten the last adult black mamba to death. It had been hiding behind a basket inside one of the villager's huts.

"David, I am scared. There are so many terrible things out there, and we have to pass right through their territory, starting tomorrow," Arlee said, shaking her head.

"We will make it, Arlee, despite them all. We simply must get home," I said with determination.

CHAPTER QUESTIONS

1. If someone close to you dies, who would you seek out to help you deal with it?

2. Besides the black mamba and king cobra, what other snakes are venomous?

3. What animal causes the most human deaths in Africa?

4. What insect causes the most human deaths in Africa?

5. What percentage of the western African rainforest is left?

6. Where is Kenya located in relation to the equator?

7. How many square miles are in the continent of Africa?

8. Should America change from the customary system to the metric system?

9. Would you like to live with Azizi's tribe?

10. What will it take to stop deforestation in Africa?

TRIVIA QUESTION

What is the largest desert in Africa?

CROSSWORD PUZZLES & GAMES

www.thevoyagers.net

Now that you have read the Chapter, answered the Chapter Questions, and researched the Trivia Question, it's time to go to our website! Click the PUZZLES tab and follow the directions. Remember, the underlined words in the chapter are the answers to the online CROSSWORD PUZZLE! You may want to write them down, as one of them is your CODE to play the online GAME!

HAVE FUN!

CHAPTER 9

"If there was concern over the cutting of trees in **Book 2, Africa**, I hate to think what has happened in the past two centuries or so since the adventure took place," Erin said solemnly.

"I just watched a National Geographic program late last night. They really show it like it is!" Drew replied. "The destruction of the natural habitat is unbelievable, and not just on the African continent. You know, Erin, I've noticed that we've become more interested in such things after reading these books."

"Yes, and I know we've learned a lot about interacting with other people, too," Erin observed. "And I just realized that there's one thing we see just about every day in school that has never been mentioned in the books."

"Oh? What's that? Drew asked.

"Bullying," Erin said.

"Wow! You're right! Can you imagine Azizi putting up with that in his village?" Drew said with a laugh. "Remember how the two would-be gold thieves were handled when they didn't conform to tribal ethics?"

"Drew, I think we need to consider how we can share these books, don't you?" Erin asked.

"I agree, but we'll talk to Dad about the possibilities after Mr. Taylor gets the copies of the books finished," Drew suggested.

"I hope it won't be much longer. We're almost finished with **Book 2, Africa**," Erin said. "Before we have lunch, let's find out what happens to Arlee and David on their way back to Mombasa. It's your turn to read. I'm not giving you any popcorn this time!"

~ Book 2, Africa ~

The Jungle

Although we wished each other a good night's rest, I do not think either one of us expected to be able to avoid tossing and turning. We had discussed our plan to put on all of our gear in the morning before the funeral service so that we would be ready to start out right after it. David agreed to meet me outside my hut after dawn.

As I came out of my hut in the morning, David was standing there, looking at everyone dressed in their brightly-colored tribal costumes. They were wearing all of their jewelry and had painted their faces with various colorful designs. Several of the tribesmen had braided their hair, incorporating assorted beads throughout. Some wore masks, but everyone was dressed in their best clothing as a sign of respect for Chief Ade. Sometime during the night, a deep grave had been dug next to the chief's hut.

Azizi came over to us and asked if we would stand close to the head of Chief Ade's grave to witness the burial ceremony that was about to take place.

Soon, six men came out of the chief's hut, holding his body above their heads. They began to walk around the people of the village. Everyone kept their heads bowed and their hands together as Chief Ade was carried by. Each person said something in Swahili out of respect.

The men then placed the great chief into his grave. He was wearing a beautiful outfit, as well as all of his jewelry, except his headband. His hands were placed across his heart, and underneath them was a beautiful necklace that his wife had made.

Azizi and his mother knelt next to the grave. Azizi placed a number of different items around his father, while his mother was chanting and crying, moving back and forth with grief. Azizi placed the skin of the black mamba under his father's feet. The skin was tied in knots and folded. After walking around to his father's head, Azizi knelt and placed his hand on his father's forehead. He began to recite the burial rites in accord with the rituals of his tribe as he looked up into the sky. Much crying was heard during this part of the ceremony. After Azizi finished, he went to his mother and helped her sit in the chair next to his.

Several of the elders in the tribe covered the body of Chief Ade with dirt. A small wooden fence that had been constructed to surround the chief's grave was put in place by the elders, completing the ceremony.

Azizi rose from his chair, and said, "It is time to gather together and hold each other's hands. My father's wishes have been carried out in accordance with the ways of his ancestors."

With everyone having paid their respect, Azizi asked that the food and water be brought out. As the villagers ate together, they were to think about the many great things that Chief Ade had accomplished in his life.

With everyone assembled, Azizi announced, "As soon as we finish eating and drinking, our new brother and sister must be on their way. The time has come for them to go back to Mombasa, and then back home. We must wish them a safe journey!"

To our amazement, many of the people of the village came to us and said, "Please stay with us." Even those who spoke no English made sure that they had someone near them who could interpret so as to express their sentiments. But with strength and determination, however, we said we had to be on our way.

I asked Azizi if I could say a few words to the tribe. He nodded and remained standing to translate.

"Never in our lives have we met a more beautiful and

compassionate group of people than yourselves. It has been our honor to be here and to be accepted by you. We have no choice but to go home, for we miss our own people. But we promise you that in every way possible, we will <u>educate</u> others about your beautiful country. David and I will tell them about the tragedy of what is happening to the people of Africa and your beautiful environment. We hope to come back and visit you again one day."

No one said a thing. They watched us with sadness in their eyes. I grabbed David's hand and walked to Azizi. He wrapped his arms around us, and although no words were spoken, we all understood the unspoken. This time, Azizi did not cry. Instead, he stood there as a chief – strong, proud, and in control.

Azizi asked us to wait as he returned to his hut to retrieve the items that he had promised us.

"I would like to have had more time to tell you additional secrets of the savanna and the jungle, but I know that you have decided to go, and I respect your wishes. Please remember the things that I have taught you. They may save your life. Now, before you go, eat and drink as much as possible," Azizi said, continuing to look out for our welfare.

We waved good-bye to everyone as we passed through the gate of the village. "Whatever you do, David, please do not leave my sight on this journey," I said almost in a panic.

"My sister, I have no plans to ever leave you, and I have one thing to say to you. You had better not dare to leave me either!" David said, being his old <u>humorous</u> self. We laughed and took one last look back at the village.

As we walked along, a sensation of confidence began to build. We were on our way home! In front of us, we saw the big boulders where the baboons foraged for food. As we got closer, we checked our gear to make sure that everything was in place.

The shields that Azizi gave us were light in weight but strong. There was one long stick that stretched the length of the shield, and another stick that went crossways in the middle. The middle stick was tied to the long stick in the middle. Four more sticks make up the outer skeleton of the shield. Each stick was tied at the end of the long pole and at the end of the shorter middle pole. A hide had been tightly stretched over the skeleton and sewn on while it was still wet. It was left to cure in the sun. When it dried, it also shrunk a little, resulting in very strong, taut shield.

As we were approaching the boulders, we heard the baboons screaming at the top of their lungs. Azizi had told us to be careful of the baboons in the morning, as that was when the males asserted their dominance. In baboon life, the leader of the pack rarely held his position for long. He was constantly challenged by other males for the breeding rights of the group.

We saw some of the larger males running after each other and fighting. We slowed our pace and tried to quietly make our way past them, but the biggest baboon ran toward me. It happened so fast that David had no time to draw his sword. All I could do was stick my shield out in front of me to try to stop the baboon. The baboon opened its huge mouth and its finger-long canines easily bit a whole in the bottom of my shield. As fast as the attack happened, it was over. The big male turned around and went back to his family, ready to take on any other males that might challenge him for his place in their society.

As we continued past the baboons, David said, "Well, I suppose you found that to be an educational opportunity!"

"David, that is not funny! I said with a frown. "That baboon was so fast. And with those huge teeth, I can see why they have few enemies."

"You are right, Arlee, and I am the one who learned a lesson. I should have had my sword out," David conceded.

As we left the baboons and began to walk into the open savanna, David did as he was told by Azizi, swishing his stick back and forth on the ground in front of him. We were in the midst of the long yellow grasses where predators could hide. There were also many bushes throughout the tall grasses. The thorny bushes stood about four meters high, and because they were thick, it was impossible to see through or over them.

Walking was easy at this point, and we stayed on a straight path by following the sun. But in the distance, the source of our worst fears came into view. Hundreds of meters away, we saw the beginning of the black jungle. Our brisk walk slowed, and our thoughts became heavy.

"Arlee, I know we are determined to make it through this part of the jungle, but no matter what happens, we need to stay close and remain alert," David said.

There was such a stark difference between the jungle and the savanna that it almost seemed surreal. The entrance to the black jungle was a wall made up of tall trees, bushes, vines, and leaves of every size and shape. David said that he remembered where we had exited the jungle on our trek with the warriors. It was apparently etched in his mind forever. We moved to the very same spot that he recalled, which was to the left of where we were standing, and we stopped. The wall of the jungle loomed above us.

"Arlee, after we pass through the jungle, we can rest by the river and make plans to cross it tomorrow. We need to check our gear and make sure that when we get to the darkest part of the jungle, we can run like the wind with our shields on either side," David said, continuing to strategize.

With all the courage we were able to muster, we took the first step in unison. The bright sunlight disappeared, blocked by the canopy of the trees far above our heads. We had just experienced the heat of the savanna, and we knew how muggy and steamy it was going to be in the jungle. We followed the small path that we were on with the warriors, but this time it was different. We saw and heard things we had not noticed before. The bottom of the tree trunks spread out in all directions, and a person could easily hide behind the roots at the bottom of the trees. Apparently, we had not noticed many details the first time because we were relying on the warriors to navigate for us.

It was not long, however, before we began to hear sounds that were familiar to us. Monkeys were flying through the treetops, using the limbs as a means of <u>transportation</u>. The jungle seemed more alive to us than ever, and our senses were on full alert.

Soon, the jungle became menacingly dark. As we continued to walk, we came upon a gruesome object that hung from the lower part of a tree. It was a <u>miniature</u> black head that was nailed to the tree by its hair. Underneath it were two sticks that made an "X."

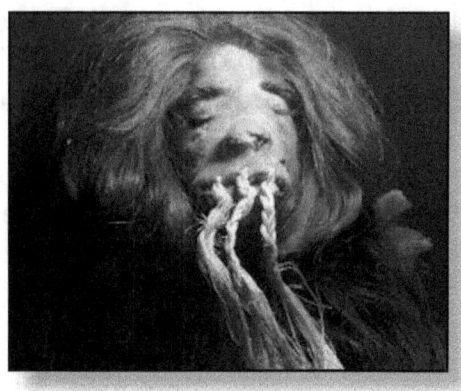

We knew what it meant. Before us was the darkest part of the jungle and a path that was full of danger.

"It is time, Arlee. We have to lock arms and hold the shields next to us on each side. We are going to run like crazy and stop for nothing. As I recall, it did not take us long to run through this part of the jungle before," David said as he extended his elbow.

I whispered, "Ready? Go!"

We took off running together, side-by-side, step-by-step. We ran as though a baboon was chasing us! Almost immediately, we heard dull thuds as darts hit our shields.

"Ouch!" I screamed.

"What is wrong, Arlee? Talk to me!" David screamed frantically.

"Oh, David, it hurts! I got hit near my ankle," I said hysterically as we kept running. "David, I feel a strange sensation. Everything is getting blurry, and I am not sure I can run anymore."

"Arlee, I will not leave you. If I have to pick you up and run with you on my back, I will," David said, gripping my arm more tightly.

As David finished his statement, I dropped to the ground and was just barely conscious of what was happening.

David did the only thing he could do, but it exposed him to the darts of the *Baka*. He put both shields over me and withdrew his sword from its scabbard. Then a strange thing happened. The *Baka* no longer shot darts at us. I realized that they already had what they wanted. They would never have be able to outrun David and me, but having stopped me with a dart, they could capture us as victims for their grisly celebration.

Even if David had fended off ten of the child-sized *Baka*, it would not have been enough. They surrounded us, and there must have been at least forty of them. David tried to communicate with these small black people as he put his sword back in its scabbard.

The *Baka* wore dark brown, v-shaped loincloths made of animal hides. All of them had knee bracelets with strings dangling down all around their legs, and their faces were painted with a variety of designs in a faint white pigment. Their bodies were painted with strange configurations in brown, green, and light yellow tones. In this part of the jungle, they were difficult to detect, even while they were standing right in front of us.

As the *Baka* stared at us, David knelt down and quickly

gave me the last of the leaves from his container. One of the *Baka* slapped the container away, but not before I had consumed the last bit of crushed leaves. Although I felt very groggy, I was glad to be <u>breathing</u> regularly. Several of the *Baka* held David and tied his hands behind his back. They did the same to my hands as I laid on the ground. To my utter horror, a number of the *Baka* picked me up and held me over their heads. When they tried to do the same with David, he started to kick them, but he was outnumbered, and they tied his ankles together, as well. They picked him up and carried both of us over their heads.

Little was said by the *Baka*, and what was said, we could not understand. After they walked a short distance, they stopped at a point next to the trail where a hidden door led to an underground cavern. All of the *Baka*, except those carrying David and me, entered the cavern. Then we were lowered down. At first, he cavern seemed to be pitch black, but the *Baka* lit a few small torches and tied both of us to the floor next to the entrance. They left one of their clan to guard us while the rest of them went down a long passageway with their torches.

As our eyes became accustomed to the dim light of the one remaining torch, David told me to take deep breaths and try to relax. My vision was still hazy, but on both sidewalls of the cavern, I began to see many shrunken heads. Most were black, but some were white. We could see that the passageway led to a room in which the *Baka* had lit many more torches. In the center of the lit room was a thick stake that appeared to reach from the ground to the ceiling. Tied to it was a monkey that appeared to be barely alive.

The *Baka* began to sing and dance around the stake. One by one, they took a sharp knife and cut a small piece of flesh from the animal. As the monkey screamed in pain, the *Baka* became even more excited. Finally, when the animal died, the *Baka* ate the rest of it. They continued dancing and singing around the stake, with one singing a phrase and the others copying what had been sung.

"How are you doing, Arlee?" David asked quietly.

"I am feeling much better, but I am so scared, David! I think I could run like the wind if we only had the chance," I whispered. "This cavern smells like blood and death!"

"I have got to think of a way out of this, Arlee," David said softly.

David was the closest to the trap door that led outside. He tried in vain to undo the ropes around his wrists. I saw him close his eyes and take some deep breaths. I know that neither of us wanted to believe that this was the end.

As I was looking at David, I saw that the trap door was being slowly opened from the outside. I heard two darts whiz by us. They landed in the neck of the *Baka* who was watching over us, and in an instant, he was immobilized. David and I looked down the passageway to see if any of the other *Baka* had heard or seen what had just happened. It appeared that all of their attention remained on their ritual.

Two warriors from Azizi's village descended stealthily and cut us free. No words were spoken as they climbed out first and extended their hands down to hoist me and then David to the outside. Above the trap door, several other warriors from Azizi's tribe were ready. They placed a heavy piece of wood across the trap door to the lair. They had already affixed a long stake at each end, having lashed them in place with vines. As they hammered the stakes at an angle into the ground, the piece of wood tightened down against the trap door. Then they piled large rocks on top of the wood. The *Baka* were temporarily trapped until more of their number came looking for them, giving David and me time to get away.

We hugged each of the warriors, and without a word, the head warrior gave us two new shields and pointed down the dark path in the direction that we needed to go. All of the warriors took off running the opposite way toward their village. David and I ran for our lives.

We made it out of the darkest part of the jungle and were coming closer and closer to the river. I saw the relief on David's face, knowing that for the moment, we were safe. When we reached the river, we finally stopped running. As we caught our breath, I walked up to David and hugged him, saying with sincere humility, "Thank you for saving my life."

"We both need to thank Azizi again!" David exclaimed.

"Yes, it will be our opening line if we meet again some day!" I said with a grin. "He was still looking out for us, even without a smoke signal!"

As the sun began to hide itself over the horizon, David took his long stick and moved some leaves aside, making a large circle. Both of us gathered wood and placed it in the center of the circle. As darkness closed in around us, we lit a fire and made sure that one end of a long sizable stick was in it. For the first time since we left Azizi's village, we were able to sit, eat a little bit of food, and drink some water.

"I should have known that we needed to repair the hole in your shield after the baboon attack. You got darted through it! That was a terrible oversight. I am so sorry," David said apologetically.

"Well, that is over with now, David," I said, knowing that he already felt badly.

"I will stand the first watch," David said. "Curl up and keep your feet well inside the circle."

I guess I fell asleep as soon as I laid my head down, because the next thing I knew, David was waking me to stand the next watch. I knew that the events of the day were replaying in his mind, so I whispered in his ear, "Relax, David. Sleep a bit. You need to be strong for tomorrow."

David said nothing as he closed his eyes and fell asleep, but his sleep was very fitful. He jerked violently, and once he distinctly said, "No!" and jolted awake briefly. I said, "It is alright, David," and he closed his eyes again. At one point, I had to lay my hands on his knees because his legs were moving up and down as though he was running. Thankfully, his sleep deepened and he did not awaken again on my extended watch.

The sun began to rise and the river started to come alive. When David awoke, he could not believe that I had let him sleep the rest of the night. He seemed slightly embarrassed that he had not stood a second watch but soon became his old self, saying, "Has breakfast already been served?" We both laughed.

We ate dried meat and drank some of the water that Azizi had given us. After checking our gear, we noticed that both water bags were getting low. It was a sobering thought, but it did not deter us in any way. We began looking for a tree that was tall enough, strong enough, and situated in the right position to be chopped down so that it would fall across the river and act as a bridge. There were a number of trees that were sturdy enough, but the bases of their trunks were too wide to cut through.

After searching the banks of the river for some time, we came across a sizable tree that did not have large roots sprawling out at the bottom of it. Without delay, David took his sword, and started <u>chopping</u> away at a particular area of the tree facing the river. He had to leave enough length and determine the angle of the fall so that the tree would span the river properly.

Before long, he was ready to start pounding wedges into the back of the tree where he had made a smaller cut. After the first couple of blows, we heard nothing, but on the third blow, we heard cracking. As David had planned, the tree fell across the river and landed on the other side, just high enough from the water so the salties could not get to us!

As David was admiring his handiwork, he noticed that what had landed on the other side was the very top of the tree where the smaller limbs were. This was the weakest part of the tree, and though it had not broken or fallen into the river, it laid precariously. If too much weight went across the tree, it could break and dislodge.

"I cannot believe it! I would have sworn that this tree was long enough to make it across the river and land on the sturdy part of the trunk instead of the branches," David exclaimed.

"David, I have seen you cut lots of trees, and few of them ever fell in exactly the same way. Look at this tree. You aimed it perfectly with your cuts, but when the tree fell, the cut end kicked back behind the stump. That made the tree land short of where you had envisioned."

"Arlee, we do not have time to look for another tree. It is already the middle of the day. We must go across this one," David said.

"I agree with you, David, and having learned from past experience, I will go first. There are no salties in sight just yet," I said with a slight smile.

"Oh, no, Arlee. That was when we had other warriors with us and pursuers behind us. There is no way that I am going to let you go first this time," David retorted.

"David, I am the lightest, and if that tree is going to hold, then I should be the one that goes first," I persisted. "Give me the rope that Azizi gave us, and when I get across, I will secure one end of it and be ready to throw it to you if necessary."

Reluctantly, David gave me the rope and said, "Please watch each step and go quickly, sister. If anything should happen, I am coming in after you!"

The rope was wound up in a circle large enough to fit over my head. With it around my neck, I wasted no time in starting across the river. The tree did not roll or move in any direction because the canopy of branches held it in place. When I was halfway across, I began to feel the tree bend as I got to the branches. Because they were extending out in all directions, it made it even harder to make progress. Below me, the giant salties had gathered.

Just as I scrambled through the branches and made it to

the other side, the tree snapped. David had his knife and sword in his hands ready to run across the trunk and kill any salty that would try to get me.

I knew that I had to scamper up the other bank quickly. Fortunately, the snapping of the tree momentarily scared the salties, and by grabbing hold of the branches, I climbed out of reach.

As I looked across the river at David, he fell flat on his back with great animation, putting his hand over his heart. Then, he jumped up and started screaming with delight. I laughed with my hands on my hips. David was amusing, but I also knew that if he was going to make it across this bridge, he would have to come up with a contingency plan.

David put his sword and knife in their scabbards and checked his gear to make sure that everything was secured. He approached the tree and put his left foot on the trunk. He looked at me, and hollered, "I have a plan! Make sure one end of the rope is tied to that tree behind you. When I tell you, throw the rest of the rope to me. We will outsmart these beasts!"

I had no idea what he was up to, but I tied the rope securely. "Alright, David, the rope is in place!" I shouted.

"Now remember, when I say throw the rope, throw it quickly," David repeated.

David was not about to tell me what he was going to do, because he knew that I would have argued. In a blink of an eye, he took off running across the tree bridge. My eyes were wide open. I could not believe what I was seeing. The closer he got to the other side, the closer the tree was to the water. Suddenly, a salty jumped up and tried to grab him, but David was too quick. A second one tried the same thing but missed. My brother was now more than halfway across, and he yelled, "Throw it!"

I threw the rest of the rope, and as he was running, he caught it in midair. Several salties were lunging at him and I could hear the loud snapping of their jaws. David was amid the tangle of branches that was partially submerged, and he pulled hard on the rope that was anchored from above. It was just the advantage that he needed to get up onto the bank, out of harm's way.

As we untied the rope from the tree, we heard a loud sound and turned around just in time to see the tree floating away.

We did not have the luxury of pondering what had just happened for long. We had to keep moving. David took the lead, watching the floor of the jungle and swishing his long stick back and forth. I stayed close behind him, looking constantly up into the trees.

With the daylight fading, we had made it more than halfway through this part of the jungle. The only thing that had slowed us down was the tree bridge. When we found a fairly open space, we started to clear out a circle. Once the fire was lit, David was in good spirits.

"Arlee, we should take two shifts apiece tonight," he began. "I will start the first shift, and then I will wake you for your shift. Please promise that when it is time wake me for my next shift, you will do so!"

"I promise, David. I am really tired," I admitted. "I am going to lay down right next to you and close my eyes, but please keep your eyes open and do not let any nasty little critters crawl on me!"

"I will have my sword ready!" he said with a chuckle.

When David woke me and said it was my turn, I checked to make sure that nothing had gotten on me. After that, I smiled and let David get some sleep. I heard so many new sounds coming from the jungle. I kept the fire burning brightly by adding logs to it from time to time. Finally, it was David's turn again. I shook his shoulder to wake him from a deep, peaceful sleep. He became alert very quickly and was more than happy to let me rest again.

The sound of my own scream was my next awareness! I

did not know how long I had been asleep, but now I was in pain again!

"Arlee!" David said excitedly. "I just slapped a scorpion off your leg and killed it. Hold still while I put a tourniquet above your knee. I am going to make a small cut where the scorpion bit you and suck out as much of the poison as possible."

I did what he asked, but the pain was getting worse. "Hurry, David. Please hurry!" I said, almost hysterically, as I held onto my knee.

David made a small slit with his knife above the place where the scorpion had stung me. He handed me a stick and suggested that I bite down on it. Then he began to suck the blood out of my leg, repeating the effort six times.

He knew he had to close the wound on my leg, so he stuck the tip of his knife into the burning hot coals of the fire. When he pulled it out, the tip of the knife was red hot. He looked at me, and we both knew that this was the only way to stop the bleeding and heal the wound. We had no more melaleuca leaves.

I bit down on the stick that David had given me as he placed the tip of his knife on the wound. I had to hold my leg still, but almost every other part of me was shaking. I wanted to scream so badly, but almost as quickly as David placed the knife on my wound, he took it off. Then, I passed out.

CHAPTER QUESTIONS

1. Can laughter be healing?

2. What animal is said to have the highest intelligence?

3. Is being physically fit like Arlee and David a good idea for you?

4. Can physical fitness enhance mental fitness?

5. What are some ways of becoming physically fit?

6. Why does the tree fall short of its intended position across the river?

7. What are some of the things that Arlee and David learn on their adventure?

8. What is the greatest threat to Rob in crossing the tree bridge?

9. To what extent can you trust a wild animal?

10. Would you be able to administer first aid to someone in need?

TRIVIA QUESTION

What is the second longest river in Africa?

CROSSWORD PUZZLES & GAMES

www.thevoyagers.net
Now that you have read the Chapter, answered the Chapter Questions, and researched the Trivia Question, it's time to go to our website! Click the PUZZLES tab and follow the directions. Remember, the underlined words in the chapter are the answers to the online CROSSWORD PUZZLE! You may want to write them down, as one of them is your CODE to play the online GAME!

HAVE FUN!

Chapter 10

"Thanks, Mom. That was a great lunch!" Drew said as Erin began to clear the dishes from the dining table. "Erin and I have been thinking about how we could share the books with our friends after the museum team completes its work."

"Needless to say, we are thrilled about Mr. Taylor's invitation for our family to meet him and his team at the cave later this afternoon!" Erin added.

"Yes, your father will be here in a couple of hours to pick us up. He said that Mr. Taylor is quite certain that the media will want to interview you two when he breaks the story to them tomorrow," Jean said to her teens.

"Just think of the possibilities!" Erin exclaimed. "Sharing the adventures with the students in the school systems, starting reading clubs, reenacting the books as stage plays – it's endless!"

"Yes, but we need to read the last chapter of **Book 2, Africa** before Dad arrives," Drew said. "There's bound to be some surprises!"

~ Book 2, Africa ~

The Stand

I patiently let Arlee sleep for awhile, but I knew we had to get out of the jungle. When I tried to wake her by nudging her shoulder, it had no effect. So, with both hands, I grabbed her shoulders and gently shook her until her eyes finally began to open.

"Arlee, we must get out of the jungle and onto the savanna as quickly as possible. Please get up and follow me."

She was still groggy, but she said, "Alright, David. I will follow you." As she tried to get to her feet, she threw up. Apparently, the scorpion had injected more poison than I had realized.

When Arlee finally stood up and began to walk, she said she felt pain in her leg. She bravely continued along, holding onto my arm, but the pain was increasing. After Arlee began to limp, she wrapped her arm across my back and over my shoulder, putting more of her weight on me.

I stopped several times for her to catch her breath, and I saw that she was sweating. Her face was very pale, and I knew that if I did not do something soon, we had no chance of making it to the savanna before sunset. I decided that I had to put her on my back.

There was no argument from Arlee as I knelt down to allow her to wrap her arms around my neck. She laid her head on my right shoulder and I pulled both of her legs to my left side so that I could still hold onto the long stick with my right hand. As I walked, I continued to swish the stick back and forth in front of us.

At first, I felt strong and made good time. But after awhile, Arlee's weight began to take its toll on my legs. I slowed down considerably, and on several occasions, I had to stop and rest, but I was determined to get to the savanna before nightfall. I remembered a trick that had Azizi taught us. It was designed to alert any predators around us, and I hoped that it would also take my mind off of what I was doing.

I started singing. At first, my tone and volume were low.

But, after awhile, I started singing with all my might. I thought to myself, I sure hope no one can hear this but Arlee. The more I sang, the lighter Arlee became and the faster I could walk.

Arlee, on the other hand, was fighting for her life, while struggling to stay on my back. She said that her muscles were not reacting to her commands, and I could hear that her breathing was becoming more labored.

With my sister's health deteriorating, the only thing on my mind was to get to the savanna. If I had to carry her all the way, I would.

The sun was making its way to the horizon, and I became desperate to get out of the jungle. I picked up the pace, stopped singing, and with the determination of a man on fire, I raced on. Finally, I saw what I had been looking for – the savanna. I was so exhausted that I could hardly move, but I put Arlee down in a safe place and began to gather wood to make a fire. I also cleared out an area next to the fire for us to sit together. When the fire reached a roar, I brought Arlee next to it.

Even though I was exhausted, I knew I had to stay awake to protect Arlee from the predators of the savanna. I made her drink some of the water that was in our bags, but she was unable to eat. I ate some of the food that Azizi had provided and drank almost half of the water that remained.

I stabbed my sword and knife into the ground next to me as the sounds of the savanna were coming closer. They were the sounds of fear, panic, and death. I stoked the fire and made sure that there was always a long sturdy stick burning at one end. Arlee looked at me with a worried expression. She could barely move her limbs. I looked back and smiled, saying, "Nice night for a stroll!" She gave me a little smile, but I also saw a tear falling.

"Arlee, try not to worry. I will take care of you. My sword and knife are ready, and nothing will get by me. I promise."

As I turned my head back toward the savanna, the hideous

laughing sound of several hyenas was coming nearer to us from somewhere in the blackness of night. It made me angry to think that these animals could create so much fear. Somehow, my body experienced a jolt of new strength. I picked up the long stick that had one end in the fire with my left hand and then put my knife between my belt and pants. With my right hand, I grabbed my sword and was ready to defend Arlee to the death. This time, I was mad, and I was ready to make good use of all the weapons I had.

As the hyenas came closer, I made sure that Arlee was as close to the fire as possible. I had made the fire long instead of round, so that the hyenas could only attack Arlee by going through me. I started yelling at the hyenas and slamming my sword against the ground. I was daring them to come closer. I wanted a chance to show them how powerful I was and how unwise it would be to attack me. I remembered that Azizi had told me that hyenas attack their prey in such a way as to confuse it, with one hyena charging from the right while another was attacking from the left.

But I was ready for whatever the hyenas would do. Suddenly, one hyena ran straight at me and I swung the long stick that was on fire. It hit the hyena in the underbelly. Sparks flew in all directions, and some of the hyena's hair caught on fire. It was enough to scare all of the hyenas for a moment. The hideous sounds of the pack quieted down, but it was not long before the sounds started again. It seemed as though the more the hyenas howled, the more courageous they became in planning their next assault.

Never taking my eyes off the hyenas in front of me, I threw more logs onto the fire to make sure that the hyenas could not attack from behind. As another frontal attack came, I slashed my sword, instantly killing one of the attacking hyenas, but even that did not seem to stop them from wanting to get to Arlee. The hyenas were becoming even more aggressive in their attempts to get to both of us. I knew that something had to change or my sister and I might well lose our lives. For the first time, fear crept into my thinking.

Then, out of the perilous black night, I heard a familiar sound. It was a sound that quieted the hyenas, and it was becoming louder and louder.

In a flash, the hyenas scattered in every direction. Arlee and I saw a huge white blur as one of the hyenas was attacked and killed. Then, one of the loudest roars that we had ever heard overruled all of the other night sounds. It was a roar that said, "I am the king!"

I fell to my knees, exhausted. "Zar! I have never been so happy to see you! Thank you for saving our lives!" I exclaimed with absolute gratefulness.

Zar appeared to understand. He came up to me and licked the back of my hand with his huge tongue that acted like sandpaper. After that, he walked over to Arlee and nudged her with his massive head. With all the strength she could muster, she turned toward him, barely able to open her eyes. Weakly she said, "I love you, Zar." Then, she closed her eyes. Zar could tell that something was wrong with Arlee, and apparently, in his own way, he knew it was his turn to help.

A deadly night turned out to be a friendly reunion, but Arlee was still in critical condition. Zar sat next to her, while I fell asleep, still sitting up.

When I awakened, I knew that I had to get Arlee to the edge of civilization as quickly as possible. Arlee was more alert after getting some sleep under Zar's powerful watch, but she still had to clench her fists in order to deal with the pain.

"Azizi taught us that lions can swim up to three miles, so Zar did not need a bridge over the river!" I said to encourage Arlee.

"Oh, that is right!" Arlee replied with a little smile.

When Zar stood up, his beautiful coat of pure white hair was stunning. He nudged Arlee and then looked up at me. When he repeated this again, I got the impression that he was offering to carry her. He got down on his haunches, and I helped Arlee get onto his back. She grasped Zar's mane and was able to hold on while fighting the pain. I bent her legs at the knees and crossed her feet at her ankles on Zar's back. Her head was resting sideways against the thickest part of his mane.

I took some of the rope that we had and looped it round and round across Arlee's back and under Zar's stomach, tying a slip-knot. I positioned myself next to Arlee, holding the back of her shirt with my right hand. I knew that I had to travel light because we were preparing to run, so I left behind my sword, knife, and shield, as well as Arlee's bow and arrows.

Once everything was ready, I said, "Go, Zar!" and the great cat seemed to understand. What a sight we were, running through the savanna.

It seemed to me that Zar could run forever. The sun was now over our heads and the heat was unbearable. I was tiring, and my legs were beginning to throb from being overworked. I considered trying to sing again but thought it might scare Zar! For the briefest of moments, I was amused at the thought of it. Instead of singing, I tried to take my mind off the pain by looking around the savanna at the herds of animals in their never-ending migration patterns.

"Oh, David," Arlee said in a weak voice. Zar and I stopped. "What is it, Arlee?" I said in a scared tone.

With all her strength, she looked at me and said, "Let me rest for a few moments, please."

Without hesitation, I untied her and helped her sit down on some soft grass. Zar sat next to her, looking all around the area and then back at her. She drank some water and had a bit of food. Her breathing was more like gasps in the terrific heat, and I noticed that her face alternated from pale white to a light red. She was dying, and I lamented that I had no melaleuca leaves left.

I was no longer mad at the salties, snakes, hyenas, or even the scorpions. The animals lived day-to-day with only two concerns – to eat and to reproduce. Unfortunately, the humans who were ravaging the land seemed to think about only one thing – killing other humans in order to overtake their land and its resources. It was very dismaying, and I began to wonder which animals and which humans were going to survive.

But right now, I was most concerned with Arlee's survival. I put my hand on her shoulder and said with conviction, "It is time to go. Are you ready, Arlee?"

"Help me get into place, please," she said softly. With Arlee secured on Zar's back once again, we took off running. The afternoon wore on, and even though I had not taken a rest since we last started running, I kept up the pace.

As I looked at Zar, my appreciation and affection for him was overwhelming. Suddenly, the great lion halted.

I looked ahead to see if I could determine why Zar had

stopped. On a small rise in the distance, I could see three men. Zar turned his massive head and looked at me. His expression seemed sad, and I understood that he could go no further.

I untied Arlee and carefully placed her on the ground. Since Zar could not be around people if he expected to survive, Arlee and I hugged him one last time. With a mighty roar and a great burst of energy, he was gone.

I knew that if these three men were evil, all that I had done was for nothing, but I had no alternative. I started yelling and waving my arms, hoping that they would see me.

Apparently, the three men had naturally directed their attention toward the sound of Zar's roar, and they saw me. As they came running, I sat down to comfort Arlee. When the men arrived, I looked up and was astonished to discover that one of them was our father!

"Oh, thank goodness! I have been looking for you two for almost three weeks. I was just starting to give up hope," Father said as he hugged me.

"Son, what is wrong with Arlee?" he said. I told him, and he immediately reached into his pocket for a container of crushed leaves. He rubbed some of them onto the area of her bite and then mixed more leaves with some water in his palm for her to ingest. Then, he laid her back down.

"Arlee, we will take you to the port and let you rest. You will be fine in a day or two." He hugged Arlee, and she said, "Thank you, Father." I stretched out my shirt above her head to protect her eyes from the sun as Father said, "We need to get off the savanna before it becomes dark, but both of you need to have some of the food and water from the men's packs before we start out."

"Father, I must ask you something," I said.

"Yes, certainly, but we need to have these good men carry Arlee back to the ship, and then you can ask me whatever you want. I have much to ask you, also!" he said.

As the men carried Arlee, they seemed to be tireless. They never said a word, and I wondered if they were Father's slaves. Finally, we made it to Mombasa, and Father's ship was in sight.

As we boarded, I noticed that there were no men in handcuffs, just men loading barrels. Since the other ships in the harbor had sailed away, we were the last large vessel there. We went below deck and got Arlee into a hammock. She seemed to be improving already!

One of the men brought a meal for the three of us and we sat beside Arlee as we had a late supper. Father asked about where we had been, and I told him all about our adventure. He was amazed, and I noticed that he even seemed to have compassion for Azizi's tribe. Finally, he said, "It was a miracle that you and Arlee made it out of there. You were very fortunate to have made friends with Azizi and his people. There are many bad things happening here in Africa, and most white people are hated."

"Father, I must tell you that the reason we left your ship was that we assumed you were making your money through the buying and selling of Africans. We saw what was happening on all of the ships around us when we landed."

At first, Father said nothing. He just stared at me. In the dim light of the cabin, I thought I saw tears in his eyes. Then he spoke.

"Son, it has been my fault for not explaining my business to you and Arlee long ago. I am getting old and can no longer take these difficult trips, so I wanted you and you and your sister to come with me this time to see what I did and to learn my trade so that you could take it over if you so desired. First, of all I would never trade human flesh. It is barbaric. I condemn it and cannot think of anything worse.

"As you know, in the last few years the British government has begun sending large numbers of criminals to Australia to alleviate the burden on their own correctional institutions. Many of these convicts are being used as slaves. Our country is becoming known for this, but many of us take tremendous pride in ourselves as Australians. I, for one, love our country and would never do anything that would be considered offensive in the eyes of our people.

"My business has been built on trading melaleuca leaves and spices, nothing more. The leaves have been proven to help people in many ways. Again, I apologize to you both for not sharing this with you earlier."

I silently looked at my father with newfound respect and affection. Finally, I said, "Father, I would be honored to learn your business in the hopes of carrying it on to the best of my ability."

As we stood up and hugged each other, Arlee arose from the hammock to join in the embrace. "I feel so much better in more ways than one!" she exclaimed. "When will the ship be leaving? We have so much to tell Mother!"

~ ~ ~ ~ ~

CHAPTER QUESTIONS

1. Would you rather be in the jungle or the savanna?

2. Would the hyenas have gotten to David and Arlee without Zar's intervention?

3. Why is it important to have hyenas in Africa?

4. Why should wild animals always be respected?

5. Have you ever been near a wild animal?

6. What are some of the negative things that are affecting Africa today?

7. What would it be like to be a slave?

8. Why do people judge others wrongly?

9. How can you avoid prejudging other people?

10. How does Arlee and David's assumption about their father's work affect them?

TRIVIA QUESTION

What is the largest waterfall in Africa?

CROSSWORD PUZZLES & GAMES

www.thevoyagers.net
Now that you have read the Chapter, answered the Chapter Questions, and researched the Trivia Question, it's time to go to our website! Click the PUZZLES tab and follow the directions. Remember, the underlined words in the chapter are the answers to the online CROSSWORD PUZZLE! You may want to write them down, as one of them is your CODE to play the online GAME!

HAVE FUN!

Mr. Will D. Rhame started his career as a Licensed Principal Broker with Shearson Lehman Brothers. While there, he founded The CPA Network Corporation (The CPA Club), which eventually became a national franchise system. The CPA Club offers continuing professional educational credits to Certified Public Accountants and attorneys. Within a two-year period, there were over 150 franchises in thirty-five states.

After selling The CPA Club, Mr. Rhame teamed up with world-renowned sportscaster, Pat Summerall, to co-author the book, ***Business Golf: The Art of Building Business Relationships Through Golf***. He also developed a sales training seminar/event for golfers of all levels, focusing on teaching participants how to play the perfect round of business golf to increase sales. His clients include IBM, GM, and The Wall Street Journal.

To complement his experience in sports, coaching, and training, Mr. Rhame became a certified Neurofeedback Technician. Utilizing a training process that enables people to change their brainwave frequencies through the use of sophisticated computer software and verbal coaching, he has helped clients with ADD, ADHD, and learning disabilities. Understanding how the right and left sides of the brain work and how to facilitate learning by changing a person's thinking patterns became the key elements in the development of Mr. Rhame's latest project – ***The Voyagers Series***.

This set of children's books is a uniquely interactive

adventure, using the technology of the internet along with an exciting, international story line. **The Voyagers Series** utilizes four different retention tools to help children not only understand what they have read but better remember the details thereof. Its aim is to change the way they learn to read, helping them to retain more and love the experience!

Mr. Rhame played college tennis, is a USPTA Instructor, has a 12 handicap in golf, and is an avid surfer. He is the proud father of three grown daughters, and he and his wife, Anna, live in Clearwater, Florida.

The Voyagers Series

www.ingramcontent.com/pod-product-compliance
Lightning Source LLC
Chambersburg PA
CBHW072137170626
46813CB00004BA/1605